'Dance if you dare,' Luca challenged softly in her ear.

'Oh, I dare,' Jen said.

Curving his mouth in one of his faint, heart-stopping smiles, Luca ordered softly, 'Prove it.'

'All right. I will,' she agreed, breaking free from his embrace.

His senses roared as Jen began to dance. The music gave her every excuse to use her body to the full, and she didn't hold back. She was hotter than hell, and every man knew it. And she was with him—which they also knew.

At the back of his mind the same doubt remained. This woman could act many parts, and one of those parts was that of the girl who had caused his brother to leave her everything.

For now it was enough to watch her dancing. The other women had joined in. He was aware of their dark, flashing eyes, seeking his approval, but he could only see Jen, like a priestess of cool, surrounded by her acolytes. Kissing her was emblazoned on his mind. He could remember exactly how her lips had felt beneath his, and how warm and soft and smooth her skin had felt beneath his hands.

Her eyes glittered invitingly with wicked promise, but was she even aware of the stir she was causing? Jen's sinuous dance moves suggested she was available for pleasure, but her fierce, flashing eyes said not. It was a challenge he found irresistible.

Susan Stephens was a professional singer before meeting her husband on the Mediterranean island of Malta. In true Mills & Boon style, they met on Monday, became engaged on Friday and married three months later. Susan enjoys entertaining, travel and going to the theatre. To relax she reads, cooks and plays the piano, and when she's had enough of relaxing she throws herself off mountains on skis or gallops through the countryside, singing loudly.

Books by Susan Stephens

Mills & Boon Modern Romance

In the Sheikh's Service
Bound to the Tuscan Billionaire
Master of the Desert

Wedlocked!

A Diamond for Del Rio's Housekeeper

Hot Brazilian Nights!

In the Brazilian's Debt
At the Brazilian's Command
Brazilian's Nine Months' Notice
Back in the Brazilian's Bed

The Skavanga Diamonds

Diamond in the Desert
The Flaw in His Diamond
The Purest of Diamonds?
His Forbidden Diamond

The Acostas!

The Untamed Argentinian
The Shameless Life of Ruiz Acosta
The Argentinian's Solace
A Taste of the Untamed
The Man from Her Wayward Past
Taming the Last Acosta

Visit the Author Profile page
at millsandboon.co.uk for more titles.

THE SICILIAN'S DEFIANT VIRGIN

BY
SUSAN STEPHENS

HarperCollins
PUBLISHERS
— Since 1817 —

First Published in Great Britain 2017
By Mills & Boon, an imprint of HarperCollins*Publishers*
1 London Bridge Street, London, SE1 9GF

© 2017 Susan Stephens

ISBN: 978-0-263-06848-1

Our policy is to use papers that are natural, renewable and recyclable
products and made from wood grown in sustainable forests. The logging
and manufacturing processes conform to the legal environmental
regulations of the country of origin.

Printed and bound in Great Britain
by CPI Antony Rowe, Chippenham, Wiltshire

THE SICILIAN'S
DEFIANT VIRGIN

For Carly.

CHAPTER ONE

'*CHE? BUON DIO!*'

Nothing could be worse than his younger brother's funeral. Until Luca Tebaldi's father hit him with a fresh disaster.

Swearing savagely under his breath, Luca closed his father's study door on the stream of mourners who had gathered in Sicily to show their fealty to the Tebaldi clan, rather than to demonstrate their grief at the loss of Luca's reckless younger brother Raoul in a senseless accident. The Tebaldis were the uncrowned kings of Sicily, but on days like this Luca's guilt at leaving his homeland as a youth ran thick and deep and ugly.

The funeral was being held on the Tebaldis' private island off the toe of Sicily, where the Tebaldi family had ruled unchallenged for a thousand years. Luca had rebelled as a youth against the lifestyle of his father and brother, believing their actions belonged to another age. His success was founded on shrewd moves in business, and legitimate takeovers. He had begged his father and brother on countless occasions to change their ways before it was too late. There was no satisfaction in being proved right.

'If all I had to worry about was Raoul's gambling debts…' The man the world still called Don Tebaldi slumped back in his leather chair, looking spent and exhausted.

'Whatever has happened, I'll put it right,' Luca soothed his father. 'You have nothing to worry about.' They might not see eye to eye, but blood was thicker than water.

'You can't put this right, Luca,' his father assured him.

'I'll fix it,' Luca stated firmly. He had never seen his father looking quite so defeated.

'As if I didn't have enough with your brother's gambling, Raoul thought it would be amusing to leave his estate to some girl he met at that casino in London.'

There was no change in Luca's expression, but his mind was whirring. His brother had been a compulsive gambler, who had increasingly distanced himself from Luca. On their last meeting Raoul had said Luca would never understand him.

'I retire to Florida soon,' Luca's father reminded him. 'You'll have to go to London to clear up Raoul's mess. Who better for the task than you, with your morally judgemental view on life?'

His father's angry gesture and the sneer on his face revealed Don Tebaldi's contempt for his sons—one too weak, and the other too strong, he would say.

Luca found it incomprehensible that a parent could feel such a level of loathing for their children. He watched as a man turned suddenly old manoeuvred his arthritic limbs behind the desk. A lifetime of excess had finally caught up with his father. He felt compassion, though they had never been close. Considering the practical side of the problem, his business interests were so successful he could easily take a break. He must. His father needed him.

'This wouldn't have happened if you had followed me

into the family business,' his father moaned as he buried his face in his hands.

'Joining the family business was never an option for me, and it never will be,' Luca said.

His father lifted his face from his hands, his expression hardening into the unforgiving mask Luca remembered so well from his childhood.

'You don't deserve my love,' he spat out viciously. 'You're not worthy to be my son. Raoul was weak, and you are worse, because you could have taken over from me, making the name Tebaldi great again.'

'I would do anything to help you, but not that,' Luca replied evenly, his mind already working on his trip to London.

His father's scornful look remained trained on his face. Neither of his sons had been blessed with his killer instinct, Don Tebaldi would tell them when Luca and Raoul were youths, as if this were a quality they should aspire to.

'You are a stubborn fool, Luca. You always were.'

'Because I won't do as you say?'

'Correct. And as for Raoul?' His father made a sound of disgust.

'Raoul always tried to please you, Father—'

'Then, he failed!' his father raged, slamming his fist on the desk to make the point.

Luca said nothing. He'd been out of the loop for a long time working on his various charitable projects. He wished he'd been around for his brother. He wished his father could show some emotion, other than hate. Even Don Tebaldi's shadowed study reeked of bitterness and disappointment in his sons, yet Luca felt compelled to offer reassurance to the older man—and he would have done, if his father's cold stare hadn't forbidden any form of human contact between them. It was an expression that lacked every shred of parental warmth.

'Leave me,' his father commanded. 'If you've nothing positive to offer, get out!'

'Never,' Luca said quietly. 'Family comes first, whether I work for the family business, or not.'

'What family business?' his father hissed bitterly. 'There's nothing left thanks to your brother.'

'There are islanders to protect,' Luca argued quietly.

'Then, you do it!' his father blazed. 'I'm done here.' Dropping his head into his hands, the once great leader began to sob like a child.

Tactfully turning his back, Luca waited for the storm to blow over. He wasn't going anywhere. Neither his father nor Raoul had ever been able to accept that he would love them, no matter what.

Luca Tebaldi could have been a worthy successor to a man who had ruled his fiefdom with a rod of iron for more than fifty years. Well over six feet tall, with the hard-muscled frame of a Roman gladiator, Luca was considered to be outrageously good-looking. With the intellect of a scholar and the keen stare of a warrior, Luca possessed the type of dangerously compelling glamour of a man born to rule. But it was Luca's steel-trap mind that had brought him such huge success. His business interests were wholly legitimate, and had been founded far away from his father's crumbling empire. Rampant sex appeal made him irresistible to women, but Luca had no time for softening influences in his life, though his late, hugely passionate Italian mother had drummed into him an appreciation of the fairer sex. Luca's raging libido was a hitch that he and his iron control had learned to live with.

His father looked up. 'How could you not know what

was happening to Raoul? You both own property in London.'

'Our paths rarely crossed,' Luca admitted. His life was so different from that of his fast-living brother. 'Is there anything more I should know before I leave for London?' he pressed, wanting to move past the histrionics to the meat of the matter.

His father shrugged. 'Raoul owed money everywhere. He left several properties, all heavily mortgaged—' These he dismissed with a contemptuous flick of his wrist. 'It's the trust fund that concerns me. *She gets that!*'

A trust fund worth millions, Luca calculated, and one of the few sources of money Raoul hadn't been able to get his hands on to fritter away. Raoul wouldn't have been able to touch the trust until his thirtieth birthday, a date still six months in the future. 'This will make Raoul's girlfriend very wealthy indeed,' he murmured thoughtfully. 'Do we know anything about her?'

'Enough to destroy her,' his father informed him with relish.

'That won't be necessary,' Luca ruled. 'Raoul didn't expect to be killed. He almost certainly drew up this will on a whim—probably after you fell out about something?' The brief look on his father's face suggested he was right. 'My brother would almost certainly have changed his intentions in time.'

'How comforting,' his father scoffed. 'What I need to know, is, what are you going to do about it now?'

'I'd rather Raoul had lived,' Luca reproached his father.

'Live to your prescription?' his father scorned angrily. 'Hard work and trust in your fellow man—who doesn't give a flying fig about you, by the way. I'd rather be dead than live like that!'

'Raoul *has* paid the ultimate price,' Luca pointed out sharply.

He'd had enough of pandering to a self-centred old man. He was still grieving for his brother, and longed for solitude so he could dwell on happier times. Raoul hadn't always been weak, or a criminal. As a child with the world at his feet, Raoul had been trusting and funny and mischievous. Luca remembered him as a wild-haired scamp, who had liked to tag along with Luca and his friends to show the older boys how reckless he could be. Raoul could swim as fast as they could, and he could dive as deep too, sometimes remaining submerged for so long that Luca had to dive down to bring him up again. It was always a prank, designed to wind Luca up, but Raoul's daring had been his entry ticket into the group. Luca and his friends had grown out of their wildness as life forced them to shoulder increased responsibility, but Raoul had never lost his lust for danger, and in one last reckless act had joined an infamous street-racing gang. He'd been killed instantly in a head-on collision between two cars. By some miracle, there were no other casualties, but Raoul's death was the most hideous waste of life.

'What a tragedy,' Luca murmured out loud as he remembered the details as relayed to him by the police officers on the scene.

'What a mess,' his father argued. 'Sometimes I think your brother's sole intention was to hurt me.'

Always the self-pity, Luca thought, but when his father's fist closed around a lethal-looking paper knife and he looked as if he might stab it into the document in front of him, which Luca presumed could only be Raoul's will, he intervened. 'May I see that before you destroy it?'

'Be my guest.' His father shoved the papers across the desk. 'Raoul's lawyer was here before the funeral. "As a courtesy to you, Don Tebaldi—"' His father mimicked a wheedling voice. 'When you and I both know he was only interested in his fee.'

'You can't blame him for that,' Luca observed as he settled down to read. 'Raoul wasn't always quick to pay his debts.' He glanced up briefly. 'And he certainly isn't in a position to do so now.'

His father's expression hardened. 'You're missing the point, Luca. The lawyer's visit was a warning. He was telling me—*me*, Don Tebaldi—not to *accidentally* misplace Raoul's will, or destroy it, as he had already cast his weasel eyes over it.'

'Raoul was free to do as he liked,' Luca commented mildly. 'This document seems very thorough. This girl must have meant a lot to him.'

'It's unlikely the girl was a love interest,' his father rapped. 'More likely, she was a clever trickster. Thanks to Raoul's mismanagement the Tebaldi family has lost most of its power and influence, but we still have enemies, Luca. How do I know that one of them hasn't put this girl up to this act of extortion?' He clutched his chest theatrically. 'I can just imagine—'

'Has she been notified of Raoul's death?' Luca interrupted.

'I asked the lawyer to hold off.' Having made an instant recovery, his father shrugged. 'I made it worth his while to do so. And she won't find out from the media. Your brother's death will hardly make the international news. Raoul would have had to make a mark on the world to do that. So yes, we can keep it quiet for now. You're still one step ahead of her. Go to London. Buy her off. Do whatever it takes—'

While his father warmed to his theme, Luca battled the ache of loss for a brother he had loved as a child, and had lost touch with as an adult. The few times they'd met recently, Raoul had mocked the way Luca lived his life, while Luca had been frustrated that Raoul couldn't seem to break free of the vicious cycle of gambling and debt. On their last meeting, he had sensed Raoul had wanted to tell him something, but hadn't felt able to confide in him. It was no use asking his father what this might have been, but maybe the girl could help. He would take the jet to London to find out who she was and what she wanted.

It was time to drill down into the facts. 'What do we know about this woman?'

Having tired of the theatricals, his father had moved on to studying the racing papers. 'She's a mouse,' he stated with confidence, glancing up. 'She'll give you no trouble. She lives quietly on her own with no money, no family, and no way to fight us.'

Luca frowned. 'The lawyer told you this?'

'I still have my contacts.' His father laid a finger down the side of his nose to demonstrate how clever he was. 'She works behind the scenes at Smithers & Worseley— the auction house that handles the high-value gemstones I collect. She makes tea there, and polishes dust off picture frames, from what I can gather, though she is studying for some fancy title or other.' His father sneered at this, but then brightened as he considered his own cleverness. 'I lost no time calling London this morning to find out what I could about her.'

Putting financial gain over the death of his son on the day of the funeral might have shocked Luca, if he hadn't known his father so well.

'I used the old charm on the chairman of the auction house,' his father recounted gleefully. 'He was only too happy to gossip with Don Tebaldi, one of his most favoured clients—'

Probably the most gullible too, Luca thought. His father was like a magpie when it came to collecting glittering gems.

An idea had begun to take root in Luca's mind. He'd read something about a fabulous gemstone with a curse on it that was due to be sold in the next few days at Smithers & Worseley. When a gem came with a curse, it was a dead cert his father would pay over the odds for it. Don Tebaldi's hidden collection was second to none. He kept his treasures hidden away on the island, where no one but he could gloat over them.

'The girl has a second job, working in a high-end bar attached to the casino where your brother used to play the tables,' his father continued, showing his contempt for the girl with a derisive laugh. 'I imagine she took the job so she could keep a lookout for men with money.'

'We don't know that.' Luca frowned. Only the facts interested Luca, and he doubted any woman with sense would make a play for a compulsive gambler like Raoul. 'I'll find her,' he promised grimly. 'You say she's a mouse, but we've no proof of that. Either way, she's going to be a very wealthy mouse, which means she can gnaw her way through the security I've put in place to protect you from the past.'

'The past?' his father derided. '*Pshaw!* Those shadows can't reach me when I've retired to Florida. I'm part of the past. I'm finished now,' he added with a wail of self-pity. 'Do what you have to, Luca. Seduce her, if you must,' he recommended, his face brightening at the thought.

Luca hummed. He had more important things to do than indulge his father's fantasies. 'I've got a better idea.'

'Then, share it,' his father insisted impatiently.

'We've got six months until Raoul's trust is released,' Luca said as he calmly calculated the facts. 'She can't get her hands on the money until then. And, just in case the lawyer has a sudden fit of conscience, I'll keep her out of his way.'

'Bring her here to the island?' his father said, catching on.

'It seems to be the obvious solution,' Luca confirmed.

His father perked up. 'But how will you persuade her to do that?'

'You'll buy another gemstone,' he said.

'Ah...' As realisation slowly dawned on his face Don Tebaldi relaxed. 'This is a brilliant solution, Luca—and one you must set in place at once. But allow yourself some fun along the way. Life doesn't have to be all about principles and caring. She may turn out to be a pretty girl, and she owes us something for the stress she's caused me.'

Disgusted, Luca refrained from comment. It was time to hunt down the mouse.

'It's Retro Night at the club!' Jay-Dee, who was usually a server like Jen at the casino, announced so loudly the club speakers howled with feedback.

For one night only Jay-Dee was MC for the annual charity event. He was in his element, Jen thought with amusement. Jay-Dee had a warm, theatrical manner, and so much verve for life, everyone loved him.

Jen thought of her friends at the casino as gloriously colourful exclamation marks in the regular pattern of her neat and ordered life. When she wasn't working in the silent intensity of the auction house, she was poring over study books with her feet so close to her three-bar electric fire in the bedsit where she lived, she was in danger of getting chilblains. Qualifying as a gemologist was Jen's goal. Her mother had been a renowned gemologist, who had passed on her fascination with treasures locked deep in the earth to her daughters. The stories she'd told them about hidden treasures when they were little girls, it was no wonder that Lyddie had grown up wanting to wear the sparkling jewels, while Jen had desperately wanted to learn more about them. She had never lost the sense of magic her mother had passed on to her, or the thought that somewhere beneath her feet there could be precious minerals, or even diamonds.

But it was Jen's job at the casino that put the chilli spice in her life, and went some way to replacing the family she'd lost. She and Lyddie had lost their parents when Jen was just eighteen. A car crash had taken them, and then the local authority had wanted to take Lyddie. Their father and mother had set such a shining example that as soon as Jen was over the worst of the shock, she was determined to keep things running as smoothly as possible for her sister. Those in authority insisted that Jen was too young to take on the responsibility of a teenage sister, but she had fought to keep Lyddie with her, and Jen's dogged persistence had finally paid off. There was no chance she would have let Lyddie go into care. She'd heard what could happen to thirteen-year-old girls, and as long as she had breath in her body no one was going to take her sister away—only fate could do that, Jen reflected wistfully.

'Reach for your wallets!' Jay-Dee's strident voice shook Jen alert. 'You know you want to!' he bellowed. 'The charity needs our help! We might need help from the charity one day—think of that!' He glanced towards the wings where Jen was standing. 'Dig deep, my friends! Our first lot...' He gestured frantically that it was time for Jen to join him on the stage. 'What will you give me for this plump rabbit, ready for the pot...?'

'Oh, for goodness' sake!' Jen exploded with laughter

as she checked her long furry ears were fixed in place. 'How am I supposed to walk on stage after an introduction like that?'

'With attitude,' one of Jen's best friends, casino manager Tess, who was standing with her, advised.

'Does Jay-Dee have to whip the crowd into such a frenzy? If this retro night wasn't in aid of such a worthwhile charity you'd never get me up there.'

The charity was particularly dear to Jen's heart. Its volunteers had helped her when her sister died. One of them had been at her side from the moment she first saw Lyddie lying in a coma in ICU, right up to the heart-wrenching memorial service for her sister.

'Raising money for this charity is the *only* reason I've allowed myself to be dressed by a sadistic corset engineer and have a powder puff stuck on my bum,' Jen said as she silently dedicated the next hour or so to the sister who would have loved nothing more than to be here in the midst of the fun to cheer her on.

'The more excitement you generate, the more they'll pay,' practical-minded Tess declared as she tweaked the bow tie she was sporting with her boxy, forties-style suit. 'You'll enjoy it once the spotlight hits you.'

'Can I have your word on that?' Jen asked wryly.

'Hop to it, bunny! Hop!' Tess commanded, miming a whip-crack.

'I feel like a rabbit trapped in headlights, while the hounds bay blue murder from the side of the road—'

'You don't strike me as anything short of a tiger—if a rather small one,' Tess conceded with amusement. 'You should be proud of your assets,' she added, casting an appreciative eye over Jen's closely bound form.

'With those lights at least I won't be able to see any of

the medallion men bidding to have dinner with me—if any of them bid, which I doubt.'

'They'll bid,' Tess assured her. 'Now, get out there and strut your stuff, Ms Wabbit!'

'What will you give me for this plump rabbit, ready for the pot?' Jay-Dee said again in a slightly hysterical tone as he glanced repeatedly into the wings.

'Here goes nothing!' Jen declared, knowing she couldn't put off her entrance any longer.

She felt exposed in the spotlight. Her satin suit was cut like a particularly revealing swimming costume. High on the leg, it left very little to the imagination, paired with flesh-toned fishnet tights, and stratospheric heels. Even Jen had to admit that with her long red hair left flowing free beneath her bunny ears the effect was startling—if a little different from her normal, understated-to-a-fault self.

'Here's to you, Lyddie,' she murmured as the stage lights blinded her.

Jay-Dee, who was dressed in garish eighties flares and platform boots, gasped with relief as he rushed to lead Jen centre stage.

'You look beeeoootiful,' he gushed as the crowd went wild.

'I look ridiculous,' Jen argued, laughing. Getting into the mood of the night, she struck a pose.

CHAPTER TWO

HIS FATHER ONLY confided in him when he wanted something, Luca reflected as he parked up outside the exclusive London club. They had never been close. Never would be close. Luca had built his own life, far away from the family compound, where he'd grown up behind razor wire with guards patrolling the grounds, with their automatic weapons ostentatiously cocked.

Tipping the valet to park his car, he pulled on his jacket, brushed back his hair, and shot his cuffs. Black diamond links glittered at his wrists. This was his London look, the passport that gained him entry to even the most exclusive Members Only club. As he approached the entrance, the door swung wide to welcome him. His first impression of the upmarket gambling den was that it was as dreary as his father's study. Subtle lighting set the mood, and, though he doubted the glass was bullet-proof, the deep shadow still reminded him of a fortress home he preferred to forget.

'Are you here for the auction, sir?' the smiling hostess asked, putting on her best smile.

'Apologies,' he said, glancing down. 'My mind was elsewhere. An auction?' he queried.

'For charity, sir—to support those with head injuries, and those who care for them, or who are bereaved.' She risked a broader smile as she gained in confidence. 'Don't think it's a depressing night—it's anything but. It's a riot in there—I'm sure you'll enjoy it.'

He doubted that. He handed her a high-value note. 'For your trouble,' he said.

'Have a good evening, sir—'

He doubted that too.

It took him a moment to adjust his gaze. If the entrance to the club was poorly lit, the interior was positively Stygian. None of the gambling tables was in operation and everyone's attention was fixed on the brilliantly lit stage, where a skimpily dressed girl, clad in a satin swimsuit with cock-eyed rabbit ears balanced precariously on top of her head, was gyrating to the pounding music, while punters called out bids to an excessively excitable MC.

'What's going on?' he asked a waiter hurrying past with a tray of drinks.

The man followed his glance to the stage. 'Dinner for two with Ms Bunny up there is on offer.'

'Thank you.' He slipped him a twenty, and then leaned back against a pillar to watch.

He understood at once why there was such interest in this particular lot. Ms Bunny had something unique about her—almost enough to make him smile. It wasn't that she was so good at what she was doing, but that she was so utterly hopeless, and that she couldn't have cared less. She had good humour in plenty, but no sense of rhythm, and even less idea of how to walk elegantly in her high-heel shoes. She was throwing herself about in a way that made him want to take off his jacket to shield her from the baying crowd—but at least they were on her side, he noticed, glancing around. His attention returned to the stage.

She felt his interest and their stares connected briefly.

A raised brow told him that a rescue attempt would not be appreciated.

There was fire beneath that costume, and it was enough to hold him to the end of her act. She was attractive, but not showy or flashy, however hard she was trying to appear so. The punters were wolf-whistling and stamping their feet for more by now, which she gladly gave them. Spotting the maître d', he remembered the reason for his mission and reluctantly pulled away from the pillar so he could ask if a Ms Jennifer Sanderson worked at the club.

'Jen's a waitress,' the maître d' confirmed. 'But not tonight,' he added, glancing at the stage. He leaned in close to make himself heard above the noise. 'For one night only, Jen's taking part in the charity auction. It's a cause very close to her heart,' he added, piquing Luca's interest. 'That's her up on the stage now,' he enthused. 'Sensational, isn't she? I've only seen Jen in her server's uniform before, or in jeans. It's surprising what a difference a pair of ears can make.'

It wasn't her ears Luca was looking at.

And his plan had just folded. Dealing with a mouse was one thing, but from the way she was handling the audience at the club he doubted Ms Jennifer Sanderson was even close to the pushover his father had imagined. She'd got all the hard-bitten punters in the casino eating out of the palm of her hand. The more she gambolled around the stage, sending herself up, the more the audience loved her. In another life she could have been an entertainer. The maître d' was spot on. She was sensational, but Jennifer Sanderson was as much a mouse as Luca.

Jen couldn't believe how high the bidding was going. 'Keep it up,' Tess advised in the loudest stage whisper ever from the wings.

Turning her back to the audience, Jen stuck out her rump and wiggled her powder-puff tail so enthusiastically it encouraged a fresh round of bidding from the crowd.

'I thought you were supposed to be a feminist,' Jen chastised Tess when she finally sashayed off stage to thunderous applause.

'I'm happy to leave my principles at the door when ten thousand is in the bag for the charity,' Tess exclaimed.

'Ten *thousand*!' Jen hugged her friend excitedly. 'I was so busy wiggling I wasn't listening to the bidding. Who on earth paid that much to have dinner with me?'

'Someone who doesn't mess around?' Tess suggested, pressing her lips together as she shrugged. 'Time to get your Miss Prim on, and start serving those hungry diners,' she added. 'They'll need something to settle them down after the excitement you've given them.'

Jen hurried off with a wide grin on her face. She couldn't wait to release her straining body from the too-tight costume. One thing that could be said for the club was that no two days were the same. She loved her job. If she didn't work here, she wouldn't hear the stories she did. Some of the customers were lonely, and only gambled to while away their lonely nights, they told her. Jen thought that, for at least some of the members, gambling was an illness, but she'd always been a good listener and credited the customers at the club with saving her when Lyddie had been fatally injured in a cycling accident. Talking to people, and having a routine to cling onto, had helped Jen to climb back from a dark hole of grief. The volunteers from the charity had told her that shutting herself away was the worst thing she could do. She had to get out and start living again for her sister's sake. Life was precious and she shouldn't waste a moment of it. They were right, hence her outrageous outfit tonight. She would do anything she could to support them after what they'd done for her.

Having exchanged the sexy satin suit for the sombre black and white uniform she wore as a server, Jen squeezed her way through the customers clustered around the bar.

'Excuse me—' She inhaled sharply as a man barred her way.

Jen's body reacted violently with approval. Too tanned and fit to be a regular at the club, he was tall, dark and swarthy, with thick, wavy black hair, and an unwavering stare. Lean and muscular, he was ferociously commanding. Maybe he was someone important. He certainly had shedloads of presence, but there was something about him that made her shiver inwardly.

He was brutally masculine. That had to be it, Jen reasoned. And she thought she knew him from somewhere. He'd been leaning against a pillar watching her dance tonight, and they'd exchanged a couple of glances—his interested, hers a warning to keep off the grass. But now she could see him close up, she wondered if she'd seen him before at the club.

'I'd appreciate having a word with you in private,' he said.

'Me?' She had been glancing round for Tess, thinking an important visitor would ask for the manager.

'Yes, you. Alone.'

He might be the most attractive man she'd ever seen, but a private interview wasn't going to happen. 'I'm sorry, but I have to work.'

He didn't take well to her flat-out refusal. As one sweeping ebony brow rose in disapproval she was already looking for a member of the security staff.

'You won't need them,' he said, as if he could read her mind. 'I don't mean you any harm.'

'I should hope not,' she said, forcing a laugh into her voice. 'Sorry, but I really do have to go now.' She stared past him towards the restaurant, but he remained like a roadblock in her way.

'I've paid a lot of money to have dinner with you.'

'Oh, it's you,' she said, remembering the ten thousand. And now she remembered why he was familiar to her.

She raised a brow as his bold stare swept over her, heating every part of her on the way. 'You're Italian, aren't you?' she said.

His eyes warmed briefly. 'Sicilian, to be exact.'

That was right. She'd got it now. 'Very glamorous,' she said distractedly as she thought what this might mean.

'Hardly,' he said.

But arrogant, she thought. Meanwhile, her body was going crazy. He exuded pheromones like room haze. Celibacy had become a habit Jen had seen no reason to break. She was certainly paying for those years of denial now.

He frowned as he angled his stubble-shaded chin to stare down at her. 'What makes you think Sicilians are glamorous?'

'Oh, you know...' She waved her hand airily. 'Sicily seems such a glamorous destination—the fabulous scenery on the island, the emerald-green sea, the sandy beaches, the Godfather—'

'That's a fantasy,' he cut in.

'I do know that. Look, is there anything else I can do for you before I go to work?'

'Yes. Confirm our dinner date,' he said.

'Well, I'm afraid it can't be tonight. I'm really sorry, but I'm sure we can work something out.' She hoped he'd take the hint and move on—arrange something with Tess, or with Jay-Dee. He didn't move. He remained squarely in her way. 'You could speak to the casino manager, Tess, about your prize. She's right over there by the door.' She turned and pointed.

'I'd rather talk to you,' he said in a way that made all the tiny hairs on the back of her neck stand erect.

There was no give in him at all, and he had paid a lot of money that would go to Jen's favourite charity. She mustn't do anything to jeopardise that.

'Just a few moments of your time,' he said with a faint smile that couldn't rub out her first impression that he looked like a pirate on a raid, though he'd shaved recently and she wasn't sure if pirates had access to razors. Nor did they wear custom-made suits, she thought, though with those shoulders she doubted he could buy anything off the peg.

'Something amusing you?'

'I'm just a little tense,' she admitted, drunk on the faintest hint of his exclusive cologne. 'I'm going to be late for work.'

'Surely, they'll forgive you this once? You have been otherwise occupied.'

'And now the auction's over, and we're short-handed tonight.'

'Pity.'

His lips pressed down in the most attractive way, and his stare was warm on her face. But…from the collar of his handmade shirt, to the tip of his highly polished shoes he radiated money, power, and success. So why was an affluent, good-looking Sicilian prepared to fork out ten thousand for a date with a waitress? Surely he could take his pick from a long line of society beauties? Or did he just have a big, charitable heart, and had happened to call in at the club by chance?

She was getting a bad feeling about this.

He reminded her of Raoul Tebaldi, a compulsive gambler Jen had come to know at the club. Everyone knew that Raoul was the son of a man who had been a notorious gangster in his day, but Jen had come to like the quiet Sicilian. She'd lost her sister, and Raoul was estranged from his family. The distance from his brother had hurt him most of all, because they had been close when they were young. This sense of loss had given them a bond, and they'd become close. Jen had looked forward to seeing Raoul each night at the club, but he hadn't been around for quite some time. A pang of dread struck her now, at the thought that something might have happened to Raoul, but, seeing the maître d' beckoning to her out of the corner of her eye, she knew she had to cut this short.

'I promise we'll have dinner another night,' she assured the Sicilian stranger.

'I can't wait long,' he said.

Jen's heart leapt in her chest, though she told herself sensibly that what he meant was that he would be leaving London soon, and not that he was impatient to see her.

'I won't let you down,' she promised.

His narrowed eyes suggested she'd better not. 'Let's make our dinner at a time and a place of my choosing,' he suggested. 'And then it will be a surprise.'

'It should be here,' she said. 'That's what you've paid for.'

'So long as we make a date before I leave,' he conceded, not wanting to put her off by appearing harsh.

'I'm sure that will be possible,' she said.

The girl was either as innocent as she looked, or she was a very good actress. Neither possibility could explain

Raoul's actions. Innocence had hardly been his younger brother's area of expertise, and if she had somehow manipulated Raoul, she could be trouble. As his father had predicted, the tragedy hadn't made the international news, so he doubted she knew his brother was dead. He couldn't be certain if Raoul had shared the contents of his will with her, but he would find out.

'You'll enjoy the food here,' she said. 'And you'll eat free.'

If ten thousand could be called free, he thought as the balance tipped in favour of her innocence. 'Eat here?' he said, frowning.

'Why not?' she said, turning her face up to him in a way that made his senses stir.

He had accompanied her to the fringes of the restaurant, but the casino was too strong a reminder of everything he'd got wrong where his brother was concerned. He wanted to leave so he couldn't see Raoul drinking too much at the bar, or throwing his money away at the tables. He had loved his brother deeply, and had longed for them to be reunited, but Raoul had pushed him away. And now it was too late.

'You won't be disappointed,' she said, misreading his expression. 'The chefs are excellent.'

'But you might like a change,' he said. 'You can go anywhere—and I do mean anywhere in the world.'

Jen was stunned. The man was wealthy enough to pay a fortune to have dinner with her for some reason, and now he was suggesting she should leap on board his billionaire bandwagon and go with him to places unknown. How stupid would she have to be to do that?

Her heart disagreed and raced with excitement. Her body wasn't much help. It looked to casting off years of celibacy with unbounded enthusiasm. Thankfully, she had more sense. He could have any woman he wanted. She couldn't remember the last time she'd had a date. It was time to get real.

'That's very kind of you,' she said politely, 'but as we've never met before, I'm sure you'll understand if I tell you that I'd feel safer here.'

'Don't you trust me?' he asked.

There was amusement in his eyes. 'I don't know you,' she said.

And then, with the charity at the forefront of her mind, she suggested, 'How about seven' o clock tomorrow evening, here? Before the club gets busy,' she explained. 'Would that suit you?' Whether it did or not, that was her best and final offer.

'I'm looking forward to it already,' he said.

There was another suspicious glow in his eyes. 'Good. So am I—and now I really do have to go.'

'Of course,' he said, turning.

She still stared at him admiringly as he walked away, transfixed by his long, lean legs, and muscular back view. It was only when he had completely disappeared from sight she realised that they hadn't even introduced themselves. So, was he related to Raoul Tebaldi, or not?

He must have put something down on paper when he bought the auction lot, Jen reasoned. No one parted with that type of money without attaching a name to it.

'Something wrong?'

She turned to see Tess, the casino manager, staring at her with concern. Tess's sixth sense where staff were concerned was unbeatable.

'He wasn't bothering you, was he?' Tess demanded as she followed Jen's stare to the door.

'No. He wanted to have that dinner tonight, and as we're short-handed I told him that I couldn't do that. Did he remind you of someone?' she added, frowning. 'Do you remember Raoul, that lonely man who used to play the tables until he had no money left?'

Tess shrugged. 'I see thousands of men come through here every year. None of them hold my attention for long, unless they complain about something. Why do you ask?'

Jen shrugged. 'No reason. And I'm probably wrong. Anyway, I do feel better having laid down some ground rules.'

'I would have done that for you,' Tess insisted. 'You only had to ask.'

'I can handle men like him,' Jen assured Tess with more confidence than she felt. 'I wouldn't deserve a job here if I couldn't...'

'But?' Tess queried, picking up on Jen's hesitation.

'But he struck me as a man who doesn't play by the rules,' Jen said thoughtfully.

'Unless he writes them?' Tess suggested.

Jen hummed. She didn't want to burden Tess with her concerns, and it was no use brooding on them. Work would take her mind off the mystery man—she hoped.

It was a relief to leave the club. He dragged on the chilly London air as if it were the purest oxygen. He felt as if his head had been under water for the past half-hour. He blamed himself for not stopping Raoul's downslide sooner. He couldn't believe he'd been so blind to his brother's troubles, or that things had got so bad.

Raoul's debts were eye-watering. He'd paid them off, dealing with an expressionless man behind a grill at the club, and then he made his donation to the charity. Next he had to unpick the story of a woman who'd just become an unlikely heiress to a fortune she knew nothing about.

He had made no final decision about Jennifer Sanderson. She appealed to him with her bold challenges and her curvaceous body. It was all too easy to imagine her clinging to his arms in the throes of passion. That might not be what he was here for, but it was the thought he carried with him from the club.

CHAPTER THREE

'DID THAT MAN I was talking to hand over the money for the auction lot?' Jen asked Tess as casually as she could at the end of the night.

'All ten thousand,' Tess confirmed. 'And he paid off his brother's gambling debts.'

'His brother?'

'Raoul Tebaldi.'

A shiver raced down Jen's spine at the thought that, just as she had suspected, the Sicilian stranger was Raoul's brother. Raoul had confided in her that he was on a downward spiral, and only wished he were still close to his brother. 'If only I could confide in Luca as I used to when we were young,' he'd said with such longing in his eyes.

Luca...

'I don't know anything more about the guy who bought the dinner with you,' Tess admitted. 'My best guess is, he'll be back to collect what he's paid for. He didn't strike me as the type to cut and run.'

'Worse luck,' Jen said, only half joking.

'Who are you trying to kid?' Tess demanded, shooting Jen a shrewd look. 'It isn't every day a man walks into the club and pays a fortune to have dinner with you—especially not one who looks like that.'

'Which is exactly why I'm so suspicious,' Jen confessed. 'Surely, I'm hardly his type.'

'He's a generous guy with plenty of money,' Tess argued. 'Why read any more into it than that? My job here is to keep everyone happy and make sure things run smoothly, while yours is to make everyone feel welcome—and no more than that. You hit the right balance beautifully, Jen, which is why you're so popular.'

All Jen could think was, what had happened to Raoul? She didn't have a good feeling about it. The coincidence of his brother buying time with her was just too strong. Why had he done that? What did he want? Had Raoul mentioned her to Luca? That seemed unlikely. Was it possible that while she'd been getting on with her life, another tragedy had been unfolding?

Friday morning, aka almost the weekend, and Jen was settling in to her day job. Officially, according to her employment records, she was a part-time student studying to be a gemologist, working in central London on day release from college, so she could gain hands-on experience of working with precious stones. In reality, she went to college three days a week, and the rest of the time she was gofer and tea lady to the distinguished ladies and gentlemen of the board at Smithers & Worseley Auction House, London

'The buyer's request is quite straightforward,' the chairman of the prestigious house had just announced.

Staring down his aquiline nose through gold half-moon glasses, Melvyn Worseley Esquire proceeded to explain: 'Don Tebaldi, our venerable client from Sicily—some of you may have heard of him?'

Sicily? Jen was now fully alert.

The chairman gave a dramatic pause, during which a chorus of critical hums rang out around the boardroom table. Everyone knew the reputation of the infamous Don Tebaldi, a man supposedly retired, but in the world he inhabited did anyone ever really retire? That was the unspoken question.

'Has requested that a member of our staff shall hand-carry the Emperor's Diamond to Sicily, where that same member of staff will create an exhibition of Don Tebaldi's private collection, having as its centrepiece the notorious stone.'

'Relieving Don Tebaldi of the need to touch the stone,' one director commented with a scornful laugh. 'He might be an old gangster, but he's just as afraid of its supposed curse as everyone else.'

The chairman paused to allow the laughter to die down. 'His son, Signor Luca Tebaldi—'

Jen's head shot up. *Luca Tebaldi!* The man she'd met at the club.

'Will be organising security,' the chairman continued, 'for both the courier of the gem, and the gem itself.' He looked straight at Jen. 'Am I correct in thinking that you passed the module for presenting an exhibition with a certificate of excellence, Jennifer?'

'What, me? No—yes. I mean, definitely yes.' Hearing Luca's name again had thrown her. Hearing it mentioned in the same breath as travelling to Sicily to put on some sort of exhibition for his father was distinctly alarming. She'd had the strongest sense of events overtaking her from the moment he'd stood in her way at the club.

'No wonder Don Tebaldi doesn't want to handle the gem,' another director commented. 'Who does? Though from what I've heard, the Don's luck has already run out.'

The cruel laughter around the table grated on Jen.

'His business has been on the downslide for some time now,' the chairman agreed, 'though these things can be reversed, and there's no reason to suppose the Tebaldis won't remain good clients of ours…'

Was that all he cared about? Jen thought as the chairman's stare rested on her face.

'For some unaccountable reason,' the chairman continued, 'Don Tebaldi has asked for you by name, Jennifer. You are to courier the stone to Sicily, and you are to display it along with the rest of his gems.'

'Me?' she said faintly.

'I explained that you were still a student,' the chairman told her to murmurs of surprise around the table, 'but Don Tebaldi has insisted. It appears that he has researched every member of staff, and, having read your college report and discovered that you are this year's top student, he has asked—insisted, actually, on hiring your new, fresh approach.'

'But I can't—'

'Yes, you can,' the chairman argued sharply. 'Don Tebaldi has amassed a priceless collection over the years, and it's a great honour for you to be selected for this task. You must think how it will look on your CV.'

And on the auction house register. The chairman did nothing that wouldn't benefit the house. But why choose a student when the world was full of experts? What was going on?

'It's all settled,' the chairman informed her briskly. 'Don Tebaldi will accept no one else but you, so you will be travelling to Sicily at the same time as the Emperor's Diamond, and when you get there you will catalogue his collection, and arrange an exhibition for him.'

This did not go down well around the boardroom table, Jen noticed. And who could be surprised when some of the leading experts in the world were seated next to her?

'Yes, I found it surprising too,' the chairman admitted, removing his spectacles to pinch the bridge of his nose. 'But then I remembered that Jennifer has a second job at the casino, and I wondered if she might have met one of the members of the Tebaldi family there…?'

Jen's cheeks reddened as everyone turned to look at her. 'I might have done,' she admitted.

'Well, I can't complain about your work here, so I can only hope you won't let Smithers & Worseley down.'

She was certainly a dab hand at making sure the lid was on the biscuit tin. Now she had to hope that the ideas that had won her the top prize at college would translate into something to please a client.

'This shouldn't be a problem for you, should it?' the chairman pressed, raising a bristly silver brow.

He didn't really care who went, Jen deduced. The chairman was only interested in the kudos of a member of his staff entering the secret world of Don Tebaldi. The chance to hear a first-hand account of treasures that had been locked away for years had blinded him to everything else. Whether he was suspicious or not over this unlikely train of events, he had decided that Jen would be the sacrificial lamb.

As for her own suspicions? Keep thinking about that glowing entry on your CV, Jen instructed herself firmly.

'I'd be happy to catalogue Don Tebaldi's collection, and organise an exhibition for him.' She had plenty of experience of organising things and people since her parents' death. Too much experience, probably, and even she couldn't deny that she was the top student in her year.

'Good. Well, that's settled, then,' the chairman said

with satisfaction. 'You're fast becoming indispensable to us, Jennifer,' he added with a self-satisfied smile at a job well done. 'Think of it as a free holiday,' he added magnanimously. 'It can be your bonus for the year.'

That didn't mean she'd get a pay rise. She'd still be catching a bus to work twenty years from now, while the members of the board would still be chauffeured to work in their Bentleys.

'You will meet with Signor Luca Tebaldi at three, here in this office,' the chairman added.

So soon?

Jen didn't hear much else for the rest of the meeting. She would have liked more time to prepare. Raoul disappearing, and now the sale of a valuable and notorious stone to the man who turned out to be his father—and Raoul's brother buying time with Jen at the club? Was she supposed to believe it was all coincidence?

'Jennifer?' the chairman said sharply. 'Are you listening to me? I was just saying that Signor Tebaldi expects to view his father's latest purchase, following which he will arrange transport details for both the Emperor's Diamond, and for you. This is a great opportunity for you, Jennifer,' he finished, shaking his head at her apparent lack of interest as he settled back.

'Absolutely,' she said, sitting up. 'And thank you so much for the opportunity.' At least she'd have chance to get to the bottom of this mystery.

For Lyddie, Jen thought, shooting her professional smile around the table.

Lyddie had only recently started her career as a model when she was killed two years ago. She had insisted on cycling everywhere in London, saying it was the easiest way to get around. At least Lyddie had got the chance to wear the jewels she had loved so much, having landed an endorsement for an exclusive jewellery house. She'd been on her way to model the next season's collection of diamonds when she was knocked off her bike. Jen would do this work in memory of those she'd lost, and make it a fitting tribute to the sister and the parents she had adored. She smiled, remembering Lyddie had never been able to pass a jeweller's window without squeaking with excitement when she spotted some rare stone their mother had described to them. The sparkling gems had become a bond between them when their mother died, reminding them of story time, and the three of them safe, and sitting close together.

'I will inform your college and ask for leave of absence, so you've nothing to worry about—especially not with the summer holidays fast approaching,' the chairman told her. 'Just one more thing,' he added, avoiding Jen's gaze. 'We must be sure to welcome Signor Luca Tebaldi with the *utmost* hospitality.'

Jen frowned at this comment. The *utmost* hospitality seemed to imply more than simply hand-carrying a precious stone to Sicily. She would be professional and polite, and that was all. If the chairman expected anything more of her, perhaps to drum up future business, he was destined to be disappointed.

'Signor Luca Tebaldi's father has been an outstanding contributor to our profits,' the chairman continued, confirming Jen's fears with a meaningful look. 'We can only hope his son will become an equally valuable client in the future.'

Jen stared around the boardroom table as talk turned to what could possibly tempt the Tebaldi family to spend even more in future sales. Rare stones were just that, the board members lamented: rare.

A prescient shiver ran across Jen's shoulders as she

tried to persuade herself that exchanging a draughty bed-sit for a trip to sunny Sicily was a great option, and that it would honour Lyddie's memory in the best way possible. But nothing was ever that simple, and this trip was full of uncertainty.

'Do you know the history of the Emperor's Diamond?' the chairman probed, tapping his pen on the desk as he looked at her.

At last, something she could be sure about. 'As it happens, I do,' she confirmed. She always took an interest in the rare stones that came through the auction house, and her studies had allowed her to spend time researching them thoroughly. 'It was once posted in a plain brown paper envelope, and yet it still reached its destination safely. I'm sure my trip to Sicily will be equally uneventful,' she said, reassuring everyone around the table, but herself.

I am that plain brown envelope, Jen thought as the chairman acknowledged her remarks with a thin smile.

Melvyn Worseley Esquire, aka the Chairman, took Jen aside later that day. With the Emperor's Diamond valued at a conservative thirty-five million, he said it was important to get everything just right. Jen couldn't have agreed more, and was glad she had confidence in her own abilities. If there was one thing she was good at, it was lighting and setting. Creating the elusive wow factor was what had won her the prize at college, the Vice Chancellor had told her when he'd handed her the prize.

'Perhaps you might want to freshen up and put on some make-up before Luca Tebaldi arrives?'

She looked sideways at the chairman. There was that subtle, or not so subtle, hint again. She would freshen up, but sluicing her face with cold water would be enough.

This wasn't a beauty pageant. It was a client coming to inspect a precious stone.

There was no chance of the elusive wow factor where Jen was concerned, Jen conceded with amusement as she smoothed her long red hair and checked her ponytail was in place. Pulling away from the sink in the ladies' room, she returned to the boardroom where the chairman was waiting for her.

'If you're short of cash,' he observed, viewing her thrift-shop outfit with dismay, 'I'm sure we can allow you a small amount of expenses. Creating a good first impression is paramount, don't you think?' he pressed, staring keenly at Jen over his gold-rimmed glasses.

She was suitably dressed for work, Jen thought, in a mouse-grey knee-length suit and white blouse. Admittedly, the blouse had been washed so many times the fabric was practically threadbare, but if she fastened the jacket...

The chairman lifted the velvet case containing the precious gemstone and, with maximum drama, he flipped the lid. Even Jen gasped. It was as if the diamond's luminance, having been contained within a dark box for so long, leapt out at them in a stunning display of rainbow light. She knew the physics was the other way around, and that without the light the stone was nothing, but at that moment, far from being cursed, the Emperor's Diamond seemed to contain some magical force. She had to remind herself that she didn't believe in things like that.

'I'm sure you will do a fine job displaying this,' the chairman said as Jen came towards him, drawn closer by the magnificent gemstone.

As she studied it Jen thought the diamond so beautiful she couldn't think of it bringing anything but good luck. It would never be locked away again, if she could help it. She remembered her mother saying that exceptional gems should be displayed to the public, and enjoyed by as many people as possible.

'Isn't it a remarkable gem?' the chairman murmured, obviously equally awestruck as they stood side by side, briefly joined in admiration of one of nature's wonders.

'And the ceiling hasn't fallen in yet,' Jen murmured tongue in cheek.

'Not yet,' the chairman agreed as they shared a rare smile.

Somewhere in the Victorian building, a door must have opened. Jen shivered as if a breeze had blown in. 'The wind of change,' she joked, trying to hide her apprehension as she took a step back from the so-called cursed stone.

The chairman had barely had time to put the diamond away when the door swung open and his guest strode in. Luca Tebaldi somehow managed to look even more impressive in daylight than he had at the club. He was taller, darker, and far more dangerous-looking than Jen remembered. Her heart thumped wildly as his stare lingered on her face. Why this intense interest? She was hardly one of nature's wonders. She was more run of the mill. And yes, they were having dinner tonight, but this appointment was for him to view the fabulously valuable stone his father had just purchased, so shouldn't he be concentrating on that?

'Signor Tebaldi,' the chairman gushed, moving past Jen to greet his guest.

Wearing a dark, beautifully tailored lightweight wool suit and a crisp white shirt, garnished with a grey silk tie, and with sapphires glittering tastefully at his wrists, Luca Tebaldi looked every bit the billionaire connoisseur. She could see why the chairman hoped Luca Tebaldi would become as lucrative a source of income to the auction house as his father before him. She watched as the two men exchanged a firm handshake, but once that was done Luca's stare switched to Jen.

'Jennifer Sanderson—the courier you requested,' the chairman said, introducing her.

Not wanting to seem overwhelmed by their guest, Jen seized the initiative. Stepping forward, she took a firm grip of Luca Tebaldi's outstretched hand. It was like being plugged into a power socket. She snatched her hand away as the chairman started talking about an upcoming auction for rare stones, but not before sparks had shot up her arm, and far more sensitive parts of her body were responding with even more enthusiasm. This was crazy. She didn't even know him. She didn't have to know him to feel that primitive response to a man as blatantly sexual as Luca Tebaldi, Jen reasoned with concern.

He felt the girl's reaction to him, and could see it in her darkening eyes. Last night she had been dressed in a skimpy and provocative costume, while today she was dressed as if butter wouldn't melt. Would the real Jennifer Sanderson please stand up?

They stared at each other with naked interest. She was as curious about him as he was about her. What was the connection between the Emperor's Diamond, Raoul Tebaldi, and Luca? she had to be thinking. She was smart. It wouldn't take her long to come up with some answers, though they might be wrong. He would keep her guessing until they got to Sicily.

Nothing was simple. He admired her, and he hadn't expected that. He had enjoyed her performance at the club. She'd given generously of her time and talent— such as it was. And she'd stood up to him afterwards.

He was intrigued to find out how she'd react to the next part of her journey.

The chairman was saying something about another auction Luca might like to attend. He shut the man's voice out, preferring to concentrate all his attention on the intriguing Ms Sanderson. Why did he find her so attractive? She wasn't conventionally beautiful, and she certainly wasn't as showy or as successful as many of the women he knew. And she definitely wasn't biddable, as women of his acquaintance tended to be, for fear of losing his favour. She was challenging and spiky and unpredictable. And he found her utterly fascinating. Her strange mix of caution and boldness had him in its grip. To inflame him even more, just one of her glances was enough to tell him that it was immaterial to her whether he approved of her or not. She might be moneyless and powerless, but her spirit was strong. So what did she know about his brother's will? And what would it take for her to relinquish her hold on Raoul's estate?

He barely glanced at the precious stone when the chairman held it up for his approval. He was far more interested in Jennifer Sanderson's face and trying to fathom what was behind that steady green gaze. Was it duplicity, innocence, professional interest, or something more?

'If you'll excuse me,' the chairman said, distracting him, 'I'm afraid I must leave you now. Another appointment,' he explained with a brief professional smile. 'I'll leave you in Ms Sanderson's capable hands.'

He raised a brow and the girl did too, he noticed. She had no interest in being a bonus to the deal, and her employer should have more sense than to suggest it.

'Jennifer has my blessing to offer you any assistance you might need,' the chairman added with an oily smile, adding to his damnation in Luca's eyes. Luca's only response was a brief nod of his head.

Jen tensed as the door closed behind the chairman, leaving her alone with Luca Tebaldi. 'So you're Raoul's brother,' she said. 'I thought so last night. I haven't seen Raoul for ages. I hope he's well?'

'My brother's dead.'

'Oh—' Jen's hand shot to her mouth. She was beyond shocked. She couldn't believe he'd just blurted it out. Was Luca Tebaldi's emotionless statement to hide his grief, or to test her?

'He was killed a short time ago,' Raoul's brother revealed.

'Killed?' Jen repeated numbly. A chill gripped her. She couldn't take it in. She gripped the back of a chair. There were no words. She was devastated. 'Did he...?'

'Did he suffer? Not as far as I'm aware. He was killed instantly in a head-on crash in Rome.'

'I'm so sorry.'

Poor, vulnerable Raoul was dead. It didn't seem possible. Her memories of Luca's brother were so clear. She knew Raoul had led a complicated life, but she had never imagined it would come to this.

'I should have known. I used to see him every night. I knew he was fragile, but—we used to talk,' she explained as Luca stared at her.

'Shall I get you a glass of water?' he enquired.

She couldn't speak, she could only gesture with her hands. She was still reeling at the thought that she would never see Raoul again.

'You met my brother in the casino?' Luca said as he poured her a glass of water.

'Yes. I never saw him anywhere else. We were acquaintances who become friends, I suppose, but Raoul had his own life, and I had mine.'

'What did you find to talk about?'

He handed her the glass. 'Anything and everything,' Jen said honestly, sipping the water. Another young life needlessly lost. Memories of the terrible day when Lyddie had been killed came flooding back. The police had been so kind to Jen, rushing her to the high-dependency unit of the local hospital with their sirens wailing where she'd found Lyddie still breathing. Still alive! Jen had thought, wanting to believe in miracles. Yes, the doctor had confirmed, her sister was still living, but her brain dead, he'd explained gently. Head injuries, he'd said when Jen had stared at him blankly. Irrecoverable brain damage, he'd said, before asking if she would consider donating Lyddie's organs. Up to then she had fooled herself that Lyddie was asleep and would soon wake up. There hadn't been a mark on her sister, just a small white bandage taped to her forehead. Jen could spend as long as she liked with Lyddie, the doctor had told her—but not too long, was the unspoken text, because decisions would have to be made—

'Ms Sanderson?'

'Sorry—' She turned to focus on Luca. He was so like Raoul, though a bigger, stronger version, as if he was the positive imagine and Raoul was the negative. 'I'm sorry. I keep wandering off in my mind. I'm just so shocked to hear about your brother.'

'Raoul confided in you?' Luca pressed.

'We used to talk,' Jen confirmed. Raoul had opened up about a lot of things, but she prided herself on her discretion.

'Did you talk every night?'

'What is this?' she challenged lightly. 'I knew your

brother, and I liked him very much. We discussed a lot of things.' She stopped and pressed her lips together, hoping Raoul's brother would take the hint.

'I apologise if I seem intrusive,' he said. 'I'm just trying to fill in the gaps.'

'I understand your sense of loss. I've been through something similar.'

'Oh?' he probed.

'This isn't the time,' she said quickly. 'I'm sorry for your loss.'

As Luca Tebaldi hummed, she wondered what he wanted her to say. His look was penetrating, and almost suspicious. Did he think she was chanting words of condolence because they were expected? She couldn't get past the feeling that this was the calm before the storm. If she only had some idea of where the storm was coming from, or what had caused it, she might be able to help him. Luca Tebaldi was looking at her as if she posed a threat of some kind, and he was the white knight who was here to save the day. But who was he saving, and from what?

CHAPTER FOUR

MAYBE HE WAS jealous of her relationship with his brother, Jen mused as the antique clock on the carved mahogany mantelpiece ticked away the seconds. She could understand his need to know. When she met people who'd known Lyddie, she had to hold back from grilling them, in an attempt to glean every tiny detail they might remember about her sister. It was as if she had to make a remembrance quilt, and every tiny scrap of information was vital because it might fill a gap.

Luca had been silent now for quite some time and, thanks to the memories he'd stirred, Jen's emotions peaked. She had never felt angry with a client before, but it was unfair of him to grill her. Raoul had needed him, and where was Luca Tebaldi then?

'Your brother missed you,' she said, breaking the tense silence. 'He talked about you all the time. He said you used to look out for him when he was young, but eventually you went your separate ways—'

'Did he tell you why that was?' Luca interrupted.

'No.' But Jen thought she knew. Now she'd had the chance to meet Raoul's brother, she had seen how different they were. Raoul had been lonely and sensitive, while Luca Tebaldi was steely, driven, and self-assured. With that amount of testosterone on the table, it wouldn't have been easy for Raoul to admit that he wanted such very different things out of life. Luca had his problems too, she suspected. He'd shut himself off from grief and emotion. She recognised the symptom, having done something very similar herself. That was a bond of sorts between them, she conceded.

'Did my brother ever talk money with you?'

'Money?' The mention of money cheapened her relationship with Raoul. She might not have much in the way of material things compared to the Tebaldi family, but every little thing she had, she'd earned.

'I lent your brother money once,' she said, feeling Luca Tebaldi needed to know the truth, or as much of it as she was prepared to tell him. 'Not much,' she added in response to Luca's sharp breath in.

'You *lent* Raoul money?'

'Yes.' And she had given Raoul her bag of groceries, Jen remembered. 'He'd lost everything at the tables. He didn't even have his cab fare home. It was only a twenty. I'm sorry. I thought you realised how bad things were.'

Luca's expression darkened.

'Raoul said he'd pay me back. He said he'd got expectations. I told him I didn't want his money—expectations or not. I said he should accept my twenty as a gift from a friend.'

She might as well have slapped him in the face. Of course he knew some of it, but Raoul hadn't confided in him for a long time. His brother had been on a downward slide for as long as Luca could remember. When he'd paid off Raoul's debts it had only led to Raoul building up more debts. Bailing Raoul out of jail had become such a regular occurrence, Luca had arranged for one of his legal team to be constantly on call, in case he was out of the country. It hurt to know he hadn't been there for his brother at the end. They'd been so close at one time, but, having been rebuffed once too often, Luca had switched off his feelings. It had taken this girl to remind him how much he had loved Raoul.

An aching sense of loss and regret gripped him. He showed nothing. For all he knew, she was just another of Raoul's disastrous liaisons. His love life was a car crash, Raoul had told him hauntingly once. But whatever Raoul's relationship with this girl, she'd been there for his brother when Luca was nowhere to be found.

'Do you mind if I call you Luca?' she asked, calling him back from the pit of despair. 'After all, if we're going to be working together...?'

'Working together?' he queried, frowning.

'We'll be working together on your father's exhibition, won't we?'

'I'll be keeping a watching brief, and that's all,' he assured her.

'I see,' she said. 'Oh, well. At least call me Jennifer—or Jen, if you prefer?'

'Which do you like?' He'd made her nervous, and that didn't suit him. With nerves came wariness, and wariness led to silence, and he needed her to talk.

'Jen,' she said.

'Call me Luca,' he offered.

'Luca,' she repeated, staring into his eyes.

He assessed her frank expression, and the freckled perfection of her heart-shaped face. She didn't know what to make of him. Her jade-green eyes were shadowed with puzzlement, though her generous mouth and the stubborn tilt of her chin continued to stir him. He recognised his body's reaction as the primal need to celebrate life in the face of death, which meant sex, though his father's suggestion to seduce Jen, if he had to, in order to get information out of her, had sickened him back in Sicily, and it sickened him now. If he seduced Jennifer Sanderson, it would be because they both wanted it.

'Jen,' he murmured, liking the sound of her name on his tongue.

He was in an agony of lust for a woman in whom he sensed so much potential. This was no mouse. His father's idea to buy her off was overly simplistic. His plan to keep Jen in Sicily until he could unravel the puzzle of her relationship with Raoul held far more promise.

He had considered the idea that Jen could lay a long-term plan that would allow her to inherit his brother's vast wealth, but it didn't seem likely. Not that she lacked in smarts, but his brother's death had been an accident, and she couldn't have planned for that. How would she respond when she realised how wealthy she was about to become? She would be rich enough to buy this auction house and everything in it. Raoul's legacy could be a fairy tale for a woman of such limited means, or it could become a nightmare, throwing Jen out of the world she knew, into a cold, hard place where money ruled and predators gathered. The least he owed Raoul was to get to know her, so he could understand his brother's motives—and maybe protect her, if he had to. That was what he would do, he decided as her wildflower scent assailed his senses.

Wherever she moved in the room, it was impossible to escape the force of Luca Tebaldi's personality. She'd always thought the boardroom a large, spacious room, but now it didn't seem nearly big enough. Where the task she'd been set was concerned, failure was not an option, and tension between them was growing She was determined to make a success of the project, so it was time to build bridges between them.

'I'm a little blunt sometimes,' she admitted. 'When I said I'd been through something similar to you, I was talking about the loss my sister.'

'I see.'

His face had softened slightly, enough for her to add, 'Lyddie was killed in a terrible accident two years ago.'

'And your parents?"

'Both dead. But your loss is more recent, and I remember how it felt when Lyddie died. The shock of her death being irreversible took me out for a while, but it did get better. The grief didn't fade, but I learned how to deal with it. I make the most of every precious day now in memory of my sister. I owe you dinner,' she said, rather than dwell on something that went too deep to discuss with a man she'd just met. 'Tonight, as we arranged?'

'Eight o' clock, your place?' he suggested.

'No. The casino,' Jen countered. 'It makes sense, as the supper you've paid for will be there.'

'Your address,' Luca argued quietly. 'I've planned a dinner at a place of my choosing.'

'I'd rather stick to the original arrangement,' Jen insisted.

'The club might be what I bought, but it's not what I want. I paid a lot of money for the privilege of having dinner with you, but I want you to enjoy it too.'

His argument was persuasive, and he could steal her breath away with just a look. She couldn't forget the charity would benefit from his money. Plus, she wanted to get to know him a little better so she could talk about Raoul.

Every reason paled in the face of sharing an evening with Luca Tebaldi, but she was still uneasy.

'The one-way system to my address is a little complicated.'

'I'll find it,' he said with a look that made her pulse race.

What had she agreed to? She wasn't exactly big on the dating scene. She had left all that to Lyddie. Jen's vivacious sister had been born with confidence when it came to men. When Lyddie had died, Jen had retreated even more into her shell. She hadn't wanted to talk to anyone about her sister's death, so hibernation had seemed a safer bet—until the charity had persuaded her that she needed to get back to work, and go out. She must socialise, they'd insisted. The more she talked to people, the more she would discover that they had problems too, and that would help her to be strong for them, until eventually she was strong for herself.

'Tonight,' Luca said, shooting her one last dark, amused look as he headed for the door.

'Aren't you forgetting something?'

'Am I?'

She glanced at the jewel case on the table. 'Don't you want to take a closer look at your father's latest purchase before you go?'

'Ah, yes,' he said. A smile tugged at his mouth. 'The cursed stone.'

Jen's body responded eagerly to the warmth in Luca's eyes as she insisted, 'It's a piece of compacted carbon: inert, and, hopefully, unaffected by all the hype surrounding it.'

'I like that.' He laughed, and it was a real laugh that reached his eyes, and warmed her even more. 'I've no interest in gemstones,' he confessed, 'beyond seeing this one safely installed with the rest of my father's haul. I remain unmoved,' he said with a grin. 'Except for the price, of course.'

'Which would move most people,' Jen agreed.

It was impossible to resist his charm, even if his cold side chilled her, Jen thought. In the short time she'd known him, Luca Tebaldi had changed her thoughts on men, if only because she would compare every man she met to him in the future.

'It's been interesting seeing you again, Signorina Sanderson, and I look forward to our supper tonight.'

So did she, Jen realised as they shared an uncomplicated, yet unexpectedly intimate look.

'Until tonight—' Luca was already gone, leaving Jen with the distinct impression that there was something about this situation she wasn't getting.

Luca would be arriving any time now. She was so excited—ridiculously so. She hadn't been on a date for— this wasn't a date. This was a charity lot he'd bought. She hated it when cold reality swamped her. Take her home, for instance. She wasn't going to be ashamed, even though he was a billionaire, and she lived in a bedsit in someone else's house. The space was small, but it was clean and it smelled good. She had been allowed to decorate and had put her own stamp on the room, with bright paint-box colours on the walls, and a rag rug she'd made herself out of scraps of material covering the worst of the bald patches on the threadbare carpet. She had added to the sparse furnishings with lucky finds from the local second-hand shops. Plastic dumpers contained the rest of her worldly possessions, along with those vital documents everyone had to keep. Framed photos of Jen's parents, and of Lyddie, took pride of place. Jen's eyes welled with tears as she stared at her sister's photograph. It had been taken just before Lyddie died, around two years ago, and was a vibrant, happy reminder of a moment captured in time. Jen had taken the photograph in the park close by. Lyddie had been acting the fool, turning cartwheels and grinning at Jen, and her face was still lit up with mischief, suggesting cruelly to Jen that she could breeze through the door at any time.

Dragging her gaze away with difficulty, Jen turned to test the soil in the plant pots on the window sill with her knuckles. Most of her specimens had been rescued unloved and neglected from various offices at the auction house, apart from one new addition: a small pink rose she'd bought in memory of Lyddie, and Raoul Tebaldi, the lonely man at the casino, as Jen would always think of him.

And now it was time to decide what to wear for the all-important date with Luca. She was not ashamed of her wardrobe, though she shopped in thrift stores most of the time, searching for vintage pieces that had escaped the eagle eye of collectors. She had picked up and discarded several items before coming to a decision for tonight. She could imagine the type of high-end restaurant Luca favoured. She couldn't compete with his million-dollar wardrobe, and so she had finally settled on a pretty, fifties-style dress from the second-hand-gown rail that served as her wardrobe. The dress was royal blue lightweight cotton, covered in sprigs of white flowers. Full skirted, it was nipped in at the waist, and had three-quarter sleeves with crisp white turn-back cuffs. Darted to show off the bust, it fastened down the front with tiny pearl buttons, and there was a belt of the same fabric cinching her waist. With its high neck and white Peter Pan collar, she felt ladylike and poised. It was certainly a change from jeans, or the mouse suit she wore at the office, and was far more modest than Ms Bunny's outfit. 'Don't judge a book by its cover' was all well and good, but people did judge, and it was crucial to get this right tonight.

The dress was armour of sorts, Jen concluded, her

pulse picking up from frenzied to frantic when the front
door bell rang, and something told her she would need
her armour tonight. Luca could be warm, but he could be
challenging too; either way she'd need her wits about her.
Snatching up a wrap, she opened the door and stood back.

'Wow,' he said, looking her up and down.

Had she got it wrong? Was the fifties outfit too much?
Was he having second thoughts? Was she?

About all of it, Jen concluded. Luca was gorgeous.
She was average. He was rich. She was poor. But he
was due his dinner, and the charity needed his money.
When Lyddie died Jen had vowed to value life, and live
it to the full. This was the perfect opportunity to make
good on that pledge.

As Luca stared past her into the house, she could
imagine what he was thinking. The house was conven-
tional. Her room was not. The blaze of colour, together
with the happy chaos of trying to decide what to wear
tonight, had left its mark. She doubted that Luca, living
in his sleek, expensive world, had ever seen anything
quite like it. Oh, well…

Girding her loins—aka hanging her structured fifties
handbag over her arm—she picked up her house keys,
and smiled at her escort.

Luca's dark stare swept over her. 'You look amazing.'

Relief. She'd got one thing right. He didn't look bad,
either. Casual dress suited him. But it was hardly the
outfit of choice for a gourmet restaurant. Relax, Jen told
herself as she led the way down the path. She halted at
the side of his car, a low-slung model, sleek, black, and
very expensive. She imagined the engine would purr and
then roar.

'Would you like me to help you in?' he asked politely.

'I'm fine, thank you.' *That mouth!* Firm and faintly

smiling, Luca's was a mouth made for sin—for softening and for teasing—

It could be a hard mouth too, Jen reminded herself. But he was on his best behaviour tonight. Polite *and* charming, she thought as he opened the passenger door and stood back. And drop-dead gorgeous. Luca had the type of masculine glamour film stars could only dream about. And those eyes could tell a thousand stories, all of them X-rated, she had no doubt. She quickly looked away, but not before he'd caught her staring. He smiled as she mused on the subject of rampant Tatars from the plains—that was what he looked like, with his tangle of wild black hair, and the imperious line of his sweeping ebony brows. Gathering the skirt of her dress, she did her best to slide into the car with grace, as if this were something she did most days. It certainly took more of a knack than stepping onto a bus, but she could handle it—

Really?

She cursed vigorously as her heel caught in the hem of her dress.

'Let me help you,' Luca offered.

Before she could refuse, he was down on his knees in front of her, freeing the hem.

I will! Oh, yes, I will—flew unbidden into her mind. She shoved it straight out again. This wasn't a game. This was deadly serious, she thought as Luca's magnetic stare lifted to fix on her face.

CHAPTER FIVE

THE SCENT OF expensive leather and hand-polished walnut embraced Jen as she settled into a ridiculously comfortable seat. Closing her door with a satisfying clunk, Luca strode around to the driver's side and climbed in. She was instantly acutely aware of him, so close she only had to reach out a little way and she could touch him. His masculine appeal seemed magnified tenfold in the confines of the luxurious vehicle.

'I can still get us a table at the club, if you'd like to go there instead,' she said on a throat that felt as tight as if someone were standing on it.

Luca's answer was to switch on the engine, proving that his muscle car preferred to roar, rather than purr. Why wasn't she surprised? Jen thought as he pulled smoothly into the slow-moving evening traffic. She tried to settle back and enjoy the ride, but she had already broken her cardinal rule by getting into the car of a man she hardly knew—and this was hardly a regular guy. And they were going where, exactly? She didn't have a clue, Jen realised with a pang of alarm as soft jazz filled the air. If Luca's choice of music was meant to relax her, it was a major fail. And now they were driving out of the city—

'Where are we going?' she asked.

'To an airfield.'

'An airfield?' Jen exclaimed. 'Why?'

'Um…' Luca flashed a bemused glance at her. 'To catch a plane.'

He might think that was funny, but she didn't. 'Going where, exactly?' she pressed in a firm tone.

'To Sicily, of course,' he said, frowning.

'Sicily?' The way he said it, you might think it was a café down the road. 'But I don't have my passport with me.'

'No problem. It's being couriered to the jet right now.'

'You've been in my room?' she exclaimed, fuming.

'Not exactly. I have people who arrange this sort of thing for me.'

Of course he did. A billionaire's contacts would be many and varied, she accepted grudgingly,

'You've been hired, and you know where the job is situated.' Luca gave a relaxed shrug. 'You might as well visit Sicily sooner as later.'

Turning the wheel, he swung onto the slip road leading to the motorway.

'But I haven't packed anything,' Jen protested. 'I didn't expect—' And even if she had, Luca's high-handed attitude was outrageous.

'I apologise for the short notice,' Luca drawled, managing not to sound sorry at all.

'Short notice?' Jen exclaimed. 'Don't you mean *no* notice? You should have warned me what you had in mind.'

'What kind of surprise is that?' He smiled.

She didn't.

'Tonight wasn't supposed to be a surprise,' Jen pointed out. 'What you bought at the auction was a quiet dinner for two at the club, and nothing more.'

'Do you always play by the rules, Jennifer?'

As Luca accelerated into the fast lane, she gathered he didn't.

'Last chance,' he said. 'Tell me if you want to go back?'

Throw everything up? That was where this would lead. She'd probably lose her job at the auction house, and that might threaten the qualification she'd worked so hard for. And she'd learn nothing more about Raoul, or Luca—in fact, she might never see him again.

'Well?' he said, glancing at her. 'What do you want to do?'

There was an exit coming up. She had about two minutes to decide—thirty seconds at the speed Luca was driving.

'I'm not kidnapping you, ' he said with amusement. 'I'm merely acting according to the security details I've put in place to protect you and my father's latest gaudy purchase.'

'The Emperor's Diamond?' She had never heard the precious stone referred to with anything other than awe.

'Please don't tell me he's bought something else?'

'I don't know,' she said honestly.

'Are you spellbound by its worth?'

'No,' she said honestly. 'Its value means nothing to me, beyond the fact that I have a duty of care towards a purchase made by a client. I'm fascinated by the gem's provenance—who cut the stone, who owned it before your father, and how it came to be discovered in the first place—that's what fires my interest.' She frowned. If Luca disapproved of his father's hobby, why had he taken time out of his busy life to come to London to set these plans in motion? 'A quick phone call was all it would have taken to warn me that you intended to fly to Sicily tonight—'

'The essence of security is silence,' he insisted. 'The fewer people who know my plans, the safer those plans will be.'

'Don't you trust me?'

'Do you trust me?' He softened this question with a faint quirk of his mouth. 'We hardly know each other, after all.'

'And your flight plan just happens to be filed?'

'My jet is always fuelled and ready.'

Of course it was.

'Surely you won't pass up the opportunity to see my father's fabulous collection of jewels? You've got around thirty seconds to decide' He was already braking.

'Your father's haul?' She couldn't resist reminding Luca of his previous comment.

Her reward was a brief grin that coated every part of her with heat. Thankfully, her brain was still working. 'Experts with years of experience would bite your hand off for the chance you've given me. So, why me, Luca?'

'I wanted your fresh take,' he said, keeping his attention firmly fixed on the road ahead.

She dug her heels in. 'Not good enough.'

'You're studying to be a gemologist, aren't you?'

'Studying being the operative word,' Jen agreed.

'But you're top of your class.'

'I'm a student. I've been sitting in a classroom with a professor teaching me. I would have thought you'd need the professor for this job, not the student.'

He shrugged. 'New ideas and a fresh approach are more important to me than some tried and tested formula.'

Or was she of some other interest to him altogether? Jen wondered. 'Will I meet your father?' The thought of a meeting with a man with such an intimidating reputation alarmed Jen, but she'd rather be prepared for it than not.

'No. He retired to Florida recently.'

So why was she creating an exhibition for Don Tebaldi? 'Won't he want the jewels with him, or at least want to see his latest purchase?'

'He trusts me.' Luca huffed a laugh without humour. 'He might not like me but he trusts me.'

A father not liking his own child was so far out of Jen's experience she couldn't get her head around it. She'd grown up safe in the knowledge that she had two loving parents, which had made their tragic passing all the harder to bear.

'My father didn't like either of his sons,' Luca explained without emotion. 'He held us both in contempt. There was only room for one bull elephant in our herd, and that was my father.'

She let the subject drop. She could feel Luca's bitterness and hurt. This was the most he'd opened up to her, and went some way to explaining why Raoul had felt so abandoned. On the face of it, this trip was a dream come true, but dreams could be deceptive, and this was happening too soon in her career. It didn't make sense when people ten years her senior would have trampled her in their rush to catalogue the treasures of one of the world's most notorious and secretive collectors. She was confident she had the ability to do the job, and she was excited to see the jewels. The thought of spending more time with Luca was exciting too, but she didn't fully trust his motives. Worse. She didn't trust herself. She had no experience of men. She was a frustrated virgin, which was the human equivalent of a powder keg waiting to blow.

'You look worried,' he said, glancing across. 'Do you want me to turn around?'

'I'd be mad to let you, when this is such a good career move,' she admitted frankly. 'Your father's collection is reputed to be second to none.'

'When it comes to hoarding, he does have the edge,' Luca agreed with irony.

'If that's all this trip is about—'

'What else would it be about?'

His brief glance plumbed deep, and her heart raced in response. 'I have no idea.' But if Luca thought that because she didn't have a fancy degree, or some proud family name, she wasn't clued up when it came to tricky situations, he was wrong. She might be inexperienced, but she had worked at the club long enough to know trouble when it came looking for her.

'I can still take you back,' he offered, slowing the car as he prepared to take the slip road off the motorway. 'I'll just keep going around the roundabout until you make up your mind—'

'My mind is made up.' Having him think that she was indecisive and weak was the last thing she wanted, professionally, or personally. She would see this through, and with all flags flying. 'I'm coming with you.'

'Good. We'll talk more on the plane,' he promised.

She was counting on it.

Luca relaxed. She didn't. How could she? Lyddie would have loved an adventure like this, Jen reminded herself. Her effervescent sister would have dived straight in, regardless of potential pitfalls. Jen had always been more circumspect in her approach, and had committed herself to something that still didn't quite ring true. To add to her concerns, she'd indulged in plenty of fantasies involving journeys to exotic shores with handsome men, but in reality she hadn't travelled out of London more than half a dozen times, and now she was going to Sicily with a man who was practically a stranger? It would be more of a tribute to Lyddie to seize this opportunity, rather than scuttle back to the auction house with her tail between her legs, she concluded. Plus, practical experience counted towards her degree, and it would never get better than this.

'By the way, where is the Emperor's Diamond?'

'Safe in the cargo hold of my jet.'

She had entered a billionaire's world, where anything and everything was possible, even spiriting away a priceless jewel into the hold of Luca's jet.

'I hope you're not frowning because you're worried about flying in the same jet as the cursed stone?'

'I don't believe in superstition,' Jen said frankly. 'I hope you don't?'

'I only deal in hard, cold facts,' Luca assured her.

This forthright Jen was as attractive to him as the Jen he'd first seen in a bunny suit—almost, Luca allowed with amusement. He was like a youth with a hard-on. Each time he thought he'd got the measure of Jen, she proved he'd underestimated her. It would take quite a stretch to imagine his brother having an affair with Jen, which reassured his male pride. Raoul had liked everything just so, and Jen was a little too much off the wall for Raoul, as Luca's brief glimpse into her colourful home had shown him. Quiet and circumspect at work, a glimpse into her private life had been enough to tell him that Jen was a homemaker, however individual that home might be. Like her off-duty dress sense, her style was quirky, and in a world of bland sameness he liked that. He liked her. She was refreshing. Jen didn't follow trends, she set her own. But Raoul had liked everything easy, and Jen was hardly that. Sexually, she intrigued him. Was she as experienced as her assurance implied?

His best guess was no. With her milky skin, red-gold hair and clear green eyes, she was certainly siren material, but Jen wasn't even remotely self-conscious about her looks. She had an alluring innocence beneath her quirky shell, and she challenged him, when no one challenged him. He liked that too.

Having turned into the airfield, he headed for the jet, and drew up alongside the steps. It was only now that Jen the bold, the wary, the unpredictable, the woman who had won his brother's trust when he had lost it, now hesitated with her knuckles turning white on the door handle.

'My take on the Emperor's Diamond is this,' she said with a slight shake in her voice.

He guessed she was playing for time. 'Go on,' he prompted, settling back. They had a little time to play with before his take-off slot became non-negotiable.

'I think it's considered unlucky because those who own it have too much, and they still want more, but for all the wrong reasons.'

That was exactly what he had always thought. Amassing more and more wealth and treasures had been the only thing his father had cared for, and Luca had always believed his father's coldness had hastened his mother's death. Now he thought his father's bitterness had grown over the years because he had loved Luca's mother, but hadn't known how to show it, and when he'd lost her his father had been lost too. Jen had made him think of things he hadn't thought about for years, and when she stared at him now he felt that clear green stare like a dart that refused to settle for anything less than the truth. 'It's an interesting theory,' he said.

'It's a fact,' she argued. 'There's nothing wrong with the Emperor's Diamond. It's people's lives that need adjusting. The gemstone is flawless and beautiful, and maybe some of those who come into contact with it are striving for that same perfection, but they're bound to be disappointed, because life is always more complicated than that.'

He gave her a long, amused look. 'Are you ready to go now you've got that off your chest?'

She gathered herself, and said, 'Yes, I am.'

'You're really invested in the work you do,' he observed as he helped her out of the car. 'Passionate, some might say.'

'They'd be right. I might not be fully qualified yet, but I'm good at what I do. It runs in the family. My mother was a highly respected gemologist, and I've been studying minerals and precious stones since I was old enough to read, and not because I had to, but because I wanted to.'

Just as she had determined to be the best when Lyddie died. The type of grief Jen had experienced, had demanded nothing less than positive action, otherwise she'd have given up, and that would have been an insult to her sister's memory.

She turned to Luca at the foot of the steps. 'When can I expect to return to the UK?'

'As soon as you've finished your work.'

Jen stared up to where the flight attendant was waiting for them. This was the moment when she had to take a final step into the future, or turn around and go back.

The luxurious cabin was arranged like a comfortable living room. Jen would lack for nothing, Luca determined. The smoother her stay, the more chance he had of Jen opening up to him so he could understand his brother's motives in leaving everything he possessed to her.

'What about my clothes—props for the exhibition?' she asked him as she gazed around her sumptuous surroundings, her eyes wide with wonder.

'My people followed the instructions of your chairman where supplies for the exhibition are concerned,' he reassured her, 'but if you do need anything else, you only have to ask. You can use the phone in the arm rest of your seat to check the inventory with my PA.' Reaching in front of her, he picked up the phone and punched in a number. 'This puts you straight through to Shirley. She's totally unflappable—'

She would need to be, Jen thought, if she was dealing with Luca on a daily basis. Shirley's nerves would need to be armour-plated.

Luca held out the phone and she took hold of it, but he didn't let go. For just a few moments cool plastic connected them, and the temptation to slide her hand just a little further until her fingertips touched his was all too real. As was leaning into his big, powerful body, instead of pulling away, as she should.

'Don't limit your request to things for the exhibition,' Luca added as the phone line connected. 'You can ask Shirley for anything you like.'

Could Shirley supply something to calm her heart when Luca was around?

Was it wrong to feel like this—breasts so heavy they felt super-sensitive each time Luca's dark gaze landed on her face? It was a relief to hear the cool tones of his PA, which, just for a few moments, allowed her to concentrate on something other than Luca.

CHAPTER SIX

As SOON AS they were airborne Luca dismissed the flight attendant and poured the coffee himself.

'Somehow I imagined you flying the jet,' Jen admitted as he settled down facing her in another of the hugely comfortable kidskin seats.

'And normally I would be, but I'd rather talk to you.'

'Really?' Her heart fluttered as she took a sip of coffee.

'Really.' A smile hovered around Luca's mouth. He settled back. 'Tell me something about you, Jen. You said you and Raoul were drawn to each other…?'

'Your brother was at the casino almost every day, so it was hard not to speak to him. I grew to like him a lot. I tried to tell him he should stay away, though it wasn't any of my business. Not that I didn't want to see him, but losing as Raoul did couldn't have been good for anyone, no matter how wealthy they were.'

'He didn't listen to you?'

She shook her head.

'I'm glad you tried. It's a relief to know my brother had someone to talk to.'

Jen exhaled slowly as she thought back. 'Raoul was worried, because he always lost so heavily. He started off by saying that one day his luck would change, but then

I think he stopped believing. I told him it was a mug's game, and begged him to take a break from the casino, but he said he couldn't, because it had become all about seeing me. I knew that was an excuse, but still—'

'Seeing you?' Luca pressed, frowning.

'Not like that,' Jen exclaimed, guessing Luca thought she'd had an affair with his brother. 'Because I understood him, but even so, I couldn't help him.'

Lost in regret, she fell silent for a while. 'Raoul still mourned his mother,' she said at last. 'You must too,' she added softly. 'Raoul said that's why you threw yourself into your business. He said you couldn't bear to stop working, because then grief overwhelmed you. He said it was the same with his gambling, and that if it hadn't been for me—'

'Yes?' Luca prompted.

'I don't flatter myself that I could have done anything more to help Raoul. I look back and ask myself if I could have done something to help him reconnect with you.' She shook her head.

'You and I both,' Luca said grimly, 'but I doubt either of us could have helped Raoul. My mother won't come back, and my father will never change. That was something both of us had to get used to, and Raoul never could.'

She sucked a sharp breath in when Luca leaned forward to take hold of her hands. His touch was strong and comforting, and also extremely disturbing.

'You were kind to my brother when you had your own grief to deal with,' he said, staring intently into her eyes. 'You lost your parents, and then your sister, but you still reached out to Raoul, and I must thank you for that.'

'There's no need to thank me,' she said, removing her hands from his before his touch addled her brain. 'I needed Raoul as much as he needed me. My sister had been dead more than a year when we first met, but the wound was as raw as if it had only been yesterday. We helped each other through. But what about you?'

'What about me?' Luca asked with faint amusement.

'You're still grieving, and you've no one to turn to. You've tried and failed to win your father's affection—'

'I don't need anyone's affection,' he said sharply.

'It must be lonely in your ivory tower.'

'My ivory tower?' he repeated with an edge of irony. 'Is that how you see me?''

'You're defensive,' she countered, 'That's why I make allowances for you.'

'You make allowances for me?' His stare scorched her.

'When Lyddie died I thought I'd never get over it, but I knew I had to try. Raoul wouldn't want your life to grind to a halt, any more than Lyddie would want me to waste my life grieving for her.'

'My life hasn't ground to a halt,' he protested.

'And yet you can spare time to act as courier to a precious stone your father won't even see, in the company of a woman you hardly know.'

'You're very suspicious,' he said, settling back.

'And you're not?' she parried. 'And as for my suspicions—wouldn't you be suspicious? You tell me your father doesn't need another precious stone, and I can't see why he needs an exhibition. If he's a typical hoarder the last thing he wants to do is share.'

'Maybe he doesn't want these things, and I do?' Luca suggested. 'Maybe I have other plans for my father's gemstones.'

'I'm sure you do,' Jen agreed. 'And I do know we're both grieving, and maybe we always will, but if I had one wish it would be that you could be straight with me.'

'If you're having second thoughts, you should have had them at that roundabout.'

'I'm not a quitter. I prefer to face my demons. I don't run away from them.'

'I hope you're not suggesting I do?' Luca commented with a sideways smile.

'Not at all,' Jen insisted. 'You're on a mission. I just don't know what that mission is, and I wish you'd tell me.'

'You've got a great imagination.'

'And I'm not stupid,' Jen said quietly.

'I never thought for one moment that you were. If anything,' he admitted dryly, 'the experiences you've had have only honed your powers of perception.'

She wondered what he meant by the double-edged compliment and shrugged. 'I'd rather have missed out on those lessons.'

'Me too,' Luca admitted.

His rueful smile tempted Jen to believe she was overreacting, and there was no conspiracy to lure her to Sicily, where she would only be doing her job. Having managed to convince herself, she felt as if the world seemed a brighter, kinder place.

Sicily! Jen couldn't have been more excited, or more wary of what might lie ahead as Luca escorted her down the steps of his jet

'Welcome to my homeland.'

'I'm thrilled to be here,' she said honestly.

The jet had landed on the Tebaldis' private island, which was a small, green outcrop of land, set like a jewel in an aquamarine sea a small way off the coast of Sicily, according to Jen's research. The airstrip was close to the sea. She could hear the rush of the surf, even from the steps of the plane. It was pitch black beyond the brilliantly lit airstrip, apart from the neat arrivals hall with its welcoming glow issuing from every window. The sky was like a carpet of black velvet overhead, littered with stars. The moon was a beacon that cast a steady light, hinting at rolling hills and forests beyond the airport. It was so warm she could discard her wrap. She stuffed it in her bag and turned her face skywards. She could smell more than aviation fuel in the air. Ozone cut through it on a sharp, cool breeze, and quite suddenly she felt incredibly optimistic. Why not, when she was here to do the job she loved?

'What do you think of it so far?' Luca asked, making her body quiver with awareness of him as he came to stand close.

'From what I can see of it?' she suggested dryly.

'It's beautiful, isn't it?' he said, staring up at the star-lit sky. 'I'd forgotten just how beautiful.'

'No light pollution,' she said matter-of-factly to fight off the tingling of a body that was wondering how it would feel to be wrapped in his arms.

'I thought you were the romantic one?' he said.

'Me? No,' she protested. They were just a few inches apart, and Luca's deep, husky tone had run straight through her body, setting up all sorts of delicious tingles, and it was all too easy to imagine the brush of his warm breath on her neck. 'But you do have a very beautiful island home—I looked it up on the Web.'

He laughed. 'You're such a pragmatist.'

'Definitely,' Jen agreed. 'Talking of which, when will I get to see your father's collection?'

'You're very eager.'

'Why wouldn't I be keen when I'm here to do the job I love?' She'd heard the edge of cynicism in his voice, and she refused to be judged guilty of something when she didn't know what that something was.

As Luca indicated the limousine waiting for them Jen determined that when she finished her work, she would return to London with her moral slate as clean as when she left the city. But when the driver pulled away from the kerb, that silent declaration faltered. Luca was sitting so close. Here's hoping I don't live to regret this, she thought as Luca settled back in his seat, his long, sprawled legs almost touching hers.

'So, what time tomorrow?' she asked as the limousine slowed outside what Luca had just explained was just one of several guest cottages on the family compound.

'Tomorrow?' he queried.

'Well, it's too late for supper now,' she pointed out. He didn't seem pleased about that. Perhaps he had imagined she'd spend the night with him.

'Spent, already?' he mocked.

'I want to be fresh for tomorrow's work,' she countered, trying not to think about Luca's lips very gently brushing hers—and the rest.

'Tomorrow morning, early,' he agreed.

She pressed her lips together to blot out all thoughts of kisses as she frowned. 'Fine,' she said. 'But what's your idea of early?'

'Breakfast at six?'

Jen didn't even blink. 'I'll make breakfast, if you like, and then we can set off together to view the gems?' She glanced towards the cottage, where the housekeeper had opened the front door to reveal a warm and welcoming glow inside the quaint stone building. 'And then you can treat me to supper tomorrow night.'

'You've got it all worked out, haven't you, Signorina Sanderson?'

She didn't miss Luca's calculating look. 'I'm organised,' she agreed. 'That's why you hired me, presumably.'

She stood her ground. He couldn't deny it, though, behind the professional manner, Jen's eyes were as full of questions as his. Once again, he had to remind himself not to underestimate the unique and very surprising legatee of his brother's will.

It was a relief to join the friendly housekeeper on a tour of the cottage and escape Luca's burning presence. Signor Luca had appointed Maria Head Housekeeper, the friendly woman told her, as many of his father's staff had left for Florida to accompany Don Tebaldi in his retirement.

Jen couldn't pretend she wasn't relieved to be spared the scrutiny of the old don, and if all Luca's employees were as friendly and helpful as Maria and Shirley, he couldn't be all bad, she reasoned.

'I feel very lucky to be here,' she said honestly, when Maria asked if she'd had a pleasant journey. 'Not that the flight was bad. In fact, quite the contrary, I had great company, and now I can't wait to start work.'

'Signor Luca is a wonderful man,' Maria agreed as proudly as any mother. 'I've known him since he was a little boy.'

This explanation piqued Jen's curiosity but Maria was keen to continue the tour.

The cosy building had a rustic charm Jen hadn't expected to find on a billionaire's private estate. The walls were natural stone, softened by colourful tapestries, while beautiful ethnic rugs in warm jewel colours covered the floor. The furnishings inside each room she walked past looked both comfortable and inviting.

'And your clothes have arrived,' Maria announced.

'Already?' Jen exclaimed.

'As if by magic,' Maria said with a smile.

It was only a couple of hours since Jen had spoken to Luca's PA. She was fast coming to realise that things worked differently for billionaires. Luca didn't have to stand in line, or wait around for things as she was used to doing. He had people whose job was to anticipate his smallest whim.

'Your bedroom,' Maria announced.

'How beautiful,' Jen exclaimed, turning full circle in the room. It seemed so big and airy, after her single bed tucked away in the corner of a bedsit.

And she could hear the sea!

The windows were open, and the shutters were back, allowing the rhythmical whisper of the waves to draw her across the room. She trailed her fingertips across the crisp white linen sheets on the big, sturdy bed, and only then realised how tired she was; tension, mostly, Jen thought, and now the desire to snuggle down and pull the sheets up to her chin was almost irresistible.

'You really didn't need to go to so much trouble for me,' she told Maria, turning. There were fresh flowers on the dressing table and a jug full of fruit juice on a tray, with a plate of home-made biscuits.

'It is my pleasure, *signorina*. You knew Raoul,' Maria said, as if that was all it took for the friendly woman to take Jen to her heart.

'Yes, I did.' Jen frowned sadly as she remembered her lonely friend from the casino.

'He was like a son to me,' Maria told her. 'I was a surrogate mother to both the boys when their mother died. I don't think either of them ever got over her death, though Luca showed his grief in a very different way from Raoul.'

'How do you mean?' Jen asked, hungry for the smallest piece of information.

Maria made a gesture with her hand that suggested it was too soon to talk about things like that, and Jen had some sympathy. They hardly knew each other, and some things were too precious to share with a stranger, but she was gaining a sense of a complex family that had been cruelly torn apart.

'I was very fond of Raoul,' she told Maria, smiling her understanding into the older woman's eyes.

'You understood him too, I think,' Maria said.

'I like to think so,' Jen agreed.

'He was like a ray of sunshine until his mother died, when everything changed,' Maria volunteered. Maria's smile died too, as if she was fighting with the urge to tell Jen something more. 'Luca was angry at the time—with his father, I mean,' Maria explained with an awkward shrug as if she'd already said too much, but then she firmed her jaw and confided, 'Their father was never kind to their mother.'

'I gathered as much,' Jen said quietly.

'You can see both boys in this photograph,' Maria added, more brightly now she'd changed the subject. She pointed to a framed photograph on the dressing table. 'Well, I'll leave you to settle in now,' she added. 'Would you like me to bring you some warm supper on a tray?'

'No, thank you,' Jen said, smiling. 'You've done more than enough for me already. I'm happy tonight with just a biscuit and a glass of juice.'

As soon as Maria closed the door she crossed the room to study the family photograph. There was a beautiful woman in the forefront of the shot, standing between her two boys. The older boy was unmistakeable, and Jen smiled in recognition. Luca looked like a real handful, though he was probably only eight or nine at the time the photograph had been taken. His ruffled hair and mutinous expression suggested he'd been dragged in front of the camera against his will. His T-shirt had ridden up at one side, while his grubby shorts ended above battle-scarred knees. His brother Raoul, on the other hand, even at such a young age, was the picture of sartorial elegance. Raoul was gazing up adoringly at his mother, and with his neatly brushed hair and angelic expression, Raoul looked like the type of son who would put his mother on a pedestal, and never give her anything to worry about. Even his spotless shorts boasted a crease down the front, while Luca's looked as if he'd been crawling around a coal mine. A man stood in the shadows behind the group. Jen guessed this was Don Tebaldi, who probably didn't want to be in the photograph at all. A man as infamous as he'd been wouldn't want to encourage too many photographs, she imagined. Shivering at the thought, she turned away, and wondered for the umpteenth time what on earth she'd got herself into.

It was when she went to pour some juice that she noticed the note tucked beneath the jug. It was an invitation to choose anything she liked from the dressing room, as it was all hers to take away or leave, as she pleased, when she left the island. The note was signed 'Shirley'.

Talk about efficient!

Wake up, Jen told herself impatiently. The note was further proof that Luca had been planning her visit to the island for quite some time.

Thunder rolled ominously in the distant hills. Luca asked the driver to stop the limousine short of the house. He needed to walk. He needed to think without distraction. He had to walk his frustration off. He could only hope that Jennifer Sanderson was suffering from frustration half as much as he. What had started as a cold-blooded plan had so quickly developed into something more. And he had never been able to trust his feelings. Right back to childhood, when he'd tried so hard to win his father's favour, and had so obviously failed, he'd thought there was no point in even trying. Emotional isolation was a better bet. No one could reach him, touch him, or hurt him, and now he supposed that habit had stuck.

He still wasn't sure what to make of Jen, and he had always prided himself on his ability to assess people quickly. It was one of his most notable strengths in business, but Jen/Jennifer, asset/threat, was still largely an unknown quantity. When she had chatted to Shirley on the jet it had sounded as if the two women had known each other for years, and that was largely thanks to Jen, who certainly had the ability to win people round. It was an admirable quality, but one that could count against her when he tallied up the points for and against the main beneficiary of his brother's will. Raoul had been needy, and Jen had conveniently been there for his brother. Was that planned? Or was it coincidence?

And then there were his personal feelings. The prospect of seducing Jen was far more tempting than showing her a hoard of sterile gems, but Jen wore her pride like a soft cloak that a man would have to be crass to remove. When the limousine had pulled away from the cottage, she had strode purposefully up the neat little path to greet his housekeeper, when he was used to women fawning over him. She'd made him realise that entitlement was a dangerous thing, because it led to expectations. He laughed out loud, remembering how she'd gambolled across the stage at the casino. She had certainly attracted his attention with that performance.

And would lose it, once he understood his brother's will. *Would she?*

He stopped and stared around. He hadn't realised he'd walked so far, he'd been so busy thinking about Jen. He was standing on the edge of the cliff overlooking the sea, and she was all he could think about.

The first thin streaks of dawn were showing on the horizon in stripes of salmon-pink. It was the main feast day on the island tomorrow, he remembered, a day that would hardly soothe his senses. With its theme of rebirth, and excess, this was the time of year when the islanders indulged themselves. As a youth he had taken it as an excuse to *over*indulge himself, though he had never needed much encouragement where that was concerned. The traditions of the feast day were many and various, as they had been contributed to by sailors of many nationalities who had anchored in one of the island's many bays. One thing remained constant, and that was the fact that around ninety per cent of the island's population was born nine months after the last mask and costume had been put away. With that sort of promise in the air it was all too easy to picture Jen whimpering with pleasure in his arms. Balanced against that was his suspicion about her relationship with Raoul.

He turned from the spectacular dawn to take the path back to the house.

What would today hold? One thing was certain. There would be a lot to pack into his favourite day of the year.

CHAPTER SEVEN

DÉJÀ-VU WAS A beautiful thing. Jen had discovered this shortly after dawn on her first morning on the island. She woke slowly, taking in every impression while she was still warm and snug in the comfortable bed. The memory she'd woken up to was like a strand of smoke, gone before she could grab hold of it, but after a few moments she realised it was the sound of the surf and the scent of the sea, reminding her of family holidays. The echo of sharing a bed with Lyddie, and both of them waking with excitement at what the day might hold, was enough to catapult her out of bed.

Crossing the room, she leaned out of the open window. Her heart pounded at the sight of the beach. And the beach wasn't empty, because Luca was striding across it towards the sea. Wearing just black swimming shorts, he was a magnificent sight to wake up to. *Get out there!* Jen imagined Lyddie whispering in her ear. She didn't need any encouragement, though she lingered to watch Luca until he plunged into the aquamarine sea. She should take an early morning swim. It would be rude not to.

His heart was aching. He hadn't anticipated such a rush of emotion, but this was his first morning on the island since Raoul's funeral. As he plunged into the sea, the dash of cold water reminded him that everything he was doing now, he'd done with Raoul, but they would never swim together, or laugh together again.

How had it come to this? How could Raoul possibly be dead?

Treading water, he glanced up the cliff path towards the guest cottage where he guessed Jen would still be fast asleep. It stung him to think she knew more about Raoul than he did. He wanted to question her and demand answers, and not just about the will, but he had no right to do that. He'd lost that right when he lost touch with his brother.

He powered out to sea, still thinking about Jen. His hunger for her refused to be subdued. Turning his face into the surf, he dived deep. He had to get rid of his energy somehow. Even the darker, cooler water couldn't help him. No matter what he did, Jen was still at the forefront of his mind, and the urge to hold her, touch her, and watch her respond as he pleasured her, was all it took to keep him painfully aroused.

The beach! At last, the beach! What was it about a beach that filled her with such excitement? Freedom, Jen concluded. Fresh air, wide spaces and the anticipation of discovering pirate treasure—or maybe just a curious crab scuttling sideways in a rock pool. The same thoughts she'd had as a child filled her now. Lyddie would have loved this.

Running barefoot towards the sea, she emptied her mind of everything but the glorious sense of freedom. She was eager for the shock of the chilly, early-morning waves closing around her sleep-warmed body. For a city dweller this was luxury indeed. The sky was blue, the sun was warm, and the sand was soft beneath her feet, and the sea looked absolutely perfect. As smooth as glass, it was as inviting as a cool bath on a hot day.

She had barely spared any time to investigate her dressing room, and had just rushed in and flung open all the drawers in a frenzy of excitement in the hunt for a swimsuit. Grabbing the first one she found, she had exclaimed with relief when she'd put it on and found it was reasonably modest, and in the nice bright blue that she loved. It fitted her perfectly too. Throwing a sundress over it, she had run out of the cottage, calling good morning to Maria, who was just arriving as she ran.

'I'll cook breakfast,' she'd called out. 'Don't you worry about it, Maria. Take the morning off—see you later!' And with that, she had run and run and run.

Stopping on the shoreline at the edge of the sparkling surf's big lace frill, she turned her face up to the sky. Closing her eyes, she dragged deep on the ozone-packed air. She was tempted to stand and bask in the warming rays of the sun a few minutes longer, but the sea was calling to her—

'Jen—'

She swung around with shock. 'Luca!' He was dripping with seawater, his bronzed body gleaming. 'You startled me.'

Black swimming shorts clung wetly to his taut, muscular thighs. His legs were lean and long, and muscles flexed on the wide spread of his shoulders. The thought of pressing against him and feeling her soft curves yield to his steel perfection shouldn't be anywhere in her mind, but it was right up there, and her nipples inconveniently peaked. Crossing her arms over her chest, she brazened it out. 'Good morning—I hope you slept well?'

'Extremely well, thank you.'

Liar, she thought, noting the dark circles beneath

Luca's eyes. It must have been hard for him coming back here after his brother's funeral, she reasoned.

'And you?' he pressed.

'I slept very well, thank you,' she confirmed, leaving out the bit where Luca had taken a starring role in all her erotic dreams. His physical presence half naked was enough to scramble the clearest of minds. 'Have you finished swimming for the day?'

'I had.'

As his face grew thoughtful, she said gently, 'You must miss Raoul. I miss Lyddie.' She gazed around. 'She would have loved it here.'

'Life moves on,' Luca said abruptly.

She didn't believe his apparent detachment for a single second. 'Sometimes it's good to remember, even if memories make us sad.'

This garnered her a long, searching look, but he made no comment.

'If you're going back in the sea, would you like to race me?' she suggested.

His answer to this was an incredulous look.

'I'm not bad in the water,' she confessed. 'But, if you don't feel up to it,' she teased in an attempt to shake him out of his dark mood.

'Not up to it?' Luca said, frowning.

He was standing within touching distance. He towered over her. He blotted out the sun. She was tiny by comparison to Luca, but no smaller in spirit, Jen determined.

'Well, I'm ready to go swimming,' she said, stepping back—straight onto the sharp edge of a shell!

As she yowled with pain Luca grabbed hold of her. His reactions were whip-fast, and suddenly she was in his arms. Pressed up hard against him was everything she had dreamed about—and everything that her sensible self should avoid. Closing her eyes, she tried to steady her breathing, and with that her imagination took flight. *Would he kiss her?*

What a ridiculous thought! Jen scowled as she quickly pulled away.

'Are you okay?' Luca asked with concern.

'I'm fine, but thanks for the save. I owe you.'

'The next time I fall over, I'll know who to call.'

His eyes were dancing with laughter, while her cheeks blazed red. Her body took some time to stop resonating to the possibility of a kiss, though that chance was long gone now. And thank goodness, she thought.

'Let me see your foot,' Luca insisted.

'I've told you—I'm fine.'

'Let me see it—'

Before she could argue, Luca was on his knees in front of her.

'Rest your hands on my shoulders,' he insisted, 'while I take a proper look.'

He glanced up to make sure she was going to do as he said, Jen presumed. *Those eyes*...and his shoulders felt so warm beneath her touch. She could feel the play of muscle beneath his tanned skin when he moved.

Taking hold of her ankle, Luca rested her foot on his thigh. His touch was so gentle it surprised her. It was a long time since anyone had shown her this sort of care, and her emotions rushed to the surface.

As he examined Jen's foot he marvelled at how tiny her feet were, and how soft. Her toenails were like tiny pink shells.

'No damage done,' he confirmed, springing up. 'You're lucky you didn't break the skin.'

'Thanks for checking,' she said brightly, and then her gaze dropped to his mouth.

She wanted him to kiss her, he guessed, but her eyes were troubled. Her body yearned for comfort, while her mind yearned for something more. 'You proposed a race?' he said, turning to face the sea. 'To that red buoy and back? I'll give you a head start.'

'What makes you think I need one?' she asked with indignation.

She turned out to be a strong swimmer, and he let her win the first leg of their race, but when they turned for shore he swam around her, diving beneath her and teasing her, as he would have teased Raoul. They arrived at the shore together, laughing as they waded through the surf.

'You're good,' she said.

'So are you,' he conceded.

'I enjoyed that.'

'So did I.' More than she knew.

'Did you bring a towel?'

'No.'

'Me neither. We'd better run,' she said. 'It's the only way to get dry.' And she was off, shrieking with excitement—until she tripped. Fortunately, he was there to catch hold of her, and he steadied her in his arms. She felt so good and warm and soft beneath his hands.

Moments passed, and then a few more as they stared at each other.

'What?' he demanded. Dipping his head, he brought his face close enough to stare into her eyes. She lifted her chin so their mouths were almost touching.

Accepting the invitation, he brushed his lips against hers. There was a long moment when Jen exhaled raggedly and he held his breath. She was so young, too young—he should stop this right now.

'Thank you,' she said, stepping back.

For the kiss? he wondered dryly. 'My pleasure,' he said with absolute accuracy.

To hell with this!

Grabbing her close, he kissed her again, and this time it wasn't a brush of his lips against hers, but a kiss between a man and a woman who wanted each other. It wasn't chaste and it wasn't restrained. With one hand in the small of Jen's back, he bound her to him as he lashed his fingers through her hair to bring her closer still. Their tongues clashed as she clung to him. He tasted her, and inhaled her sweet wildflower scent as he imprinted the feel of her warm body on his hands.

Sounds of need poured from her throat, as if all the emotion she'd bottled up for years had come pouring out. The same went for him. Touch, taste, scent and longing, his senses were fully engaged, and in overdrive. Jen's level of hunger surprised him. He had to remind himself that she was vulnerable, and her emotions were raw, but even that didn't work, and he allowed her to press herself against him, move against him, rub against him, until he was almost going mad, while she clung to him as if her life depended on it.

Only the urge to take things through to their final conclusion fired a sufficient warning in his head.

'Take another swim—cool off,' he recommended, pulling away.

She stood, visibly trembling, her eyes shooting daggers at him, but she said nothing in reply.

'There won't be any work today—it's a holiday,' he explained. 'Take your time. Enjoy the water. Why not?' he asked when she frowned.

'You might be here on holiday,' she began.

'The entire island is on holiday. There'll be plenty of time for you to do your work. Today everyone's in town celebrating, including me. And you,' he added firmly. 'We're both going to cut loose for a few hours.'

'Cut loose?' she said.

I've felt your hunger, and I've seen it, he thought. 'I've seen you dance at the casino, so I know you haven't forgotten how to enjoy yourself.'

Her cheeks blazed red at the memory, and then she licked her lips, still swollen from his kisses, and her eyes darkened, but not with embarrassment, he thought.

'Will we be going to town together?' she asked.

'I'll see you there. I've got things to do first. You'll have to wait for me,' he murmured, teasing her with a curving smile.

'Oh, I can wait,' she said coolly.

'Good. Enjoy the water,' he added as he headed back to the house.

CHAPTER EIGHT

SHE SWAM AND SWAM, but nothing helped to erase the fact that Luca had kissed her, and she had kissed him back. Her lips still felt sensitive. His kisses were indescribable: power, pleasure and promise combined, like nothing she'd ever experienced before. And now her body just wouldn't come down again. Even the chilly surf was no help at all. She had to stop thinking about it, but how? Luca could have anyone he wanted. He could have seduced her on the spot. She must never put herself in such a compromising position again.

Her body disagreed, and ached for him. It didn't matter how many times she reminded herself that she was here to work, and that at best she was a moment's distraction for Luca, she couldn't forget the look on his face just before he'd kissed her, *that dark fire in his eyes*, or how she'd felt when he had...

She almost choked on the thought, and managed to swallow a great gulp of water, but at least it shook her round. Work might be out of the question today, but the sun was shining and it was a special day on the island, and she had the whole day ahead of her. She just had to forget about Luca.

Forget Luca?

She'd avoid him in town, Jen planned as she waded

through the shallows. She'd go to town with Maria, and stay with her all day. Simple.

She ran back to the guest house, basking in the heat of the sun. She loved Sicily already. There was such a sense of freedom here, and anything seemed possible. Standing on the top of the cliff, she turned full circle with her arms outstretched. She had never felt better, or more alive.

Luca's kiss was the reason.

Luca's kiss was just one of those crazy things, she argued with her overly romantic inner voice. It would never happen again. She was hardly bedmate material for a sophisticated billionaire. Luca had acted on impulse as she had. It didn't mean anything beyond the fact that their emotions had been in tune for a few seconds. Those emotions had been locked up for a long time, so the consequences had been unexpected for both of them, she suspected.

She could excuse those kisses away all she liked, but they still made her feel as if she'd found her wings.

Just the idea of a very special feast day sounded decadent, Jen thought as she approached the town with Maria. Luca's friendly housekeeper had been kind enough to lend Jen a few pieces of costume, including a mask, so she wouldn't feel left out.

Decadent? She'd had no idea, Jen concluded when they drew close enough to hear the noise of the crowd and the clash of the competing bands. She didn't feel out of place in her mask, as everyone was wearing elaborate costumes, and some were quite revealing. Decadence was key, obviously. Catching sight of herself in a shop window, Jen smiled to herself, concluding that with her neat little sundress and pussycat mask she looked more like an escapee from a Beatrix Potter story, which wasn't quite the result she'd been aiming for, but if Maria was okay with it, then so was she.

All age groups were represented in town, and the dancing on the improvised dance floor in the square was already wild and furious. Some of the couples made it seem like the prelude to a fertility rite from some earlier and more dissolute age. She envied them their abandon. The music was infectious, and even her clumsy feet were itching to dance.

She paused in the shadow of a doorway to watch, while Maria went on ahead to join her friends. She felt safe and anonymous in the shadows—except for her red hair, which, even though she'd bundled it on top of her head in the messiest up-do this side of hedge, still stood out in a sea of dark flashing eyes and flowing ebony locks.

'Why, Signorina Sanderson, imagine seeing you here—'

Jen's heart turned over. The sexy drawl was unmistakeable. She warned herself to act cool, though her lips seemed to grow more sensitive just having Luca close by. Her body heated up and her heart started racing, which went against everything she had determined she would be around him.

'Oh, hello,' she said coolly.

She turned and her heart rocketed off the scale. In a black brigand's mask, Luca looked like more like a dark angel than a respectable billionaire. With his flashing black eyes and thick, wavy hair, and the stubble that had scraped her face so recently...

There weren't many men who could play dress-up and look as hard and as sexy as Luca Tebaldi. Banged-up jeans and a casual shirt with the sleeves rolled up looked so good on him. He only had to ease onto one tight hip for her world to start moving really slowly. Who would want to rush through a moment like that? His forearms were impossibly powerful. Tanned and dusted with just the right amount of jet-black hair. She could so easily imagine them banded around her. When he planted one fist on the door above her head she even thought the black leather wristband on his wrist was sexy. It was a band on a wrist, and the wrist led to a hand, she told herself sensibly. The feast day must have her in its grip, Jen concluded.

'Would you like to dance?'

'Dance?' She gave him a look. 'Have you seen me dance?'

'I have, as it happens—at the club,' he reminded her, humour glittering darkly in his eyes. 'You were great.'

'I was lousy.'

'With me you'll be better. It's not so hard,' he said when she pulled a face. 'I'll lead. You follow—'

'You think?'

He laughed.

'Oh, well, I guess that's why everyone's here,' she said, glancing around to hide the fact that she wanted to dance with him more than anything. She could still feel his arms around her, and remembered how great it felt to be the focus of his interest.

'It's just a dance, Jen. I'd hate you to feel left out.'

'I'm sure you would,' she agreed with a lift of her brow. 'Don't worry about me. I'm fine watching from here. Or maybe over there,' she amended, staring across the square in the interest of trying to put some safety space between them.

'Would you like me to escort you?' Luca asked.

All the women were flashing him heated glances as Luca pushed his strong, tanned hands through his unruly hair—which only succeeded in tangling it all the more. 'Something troubling you?' he pressed. His eyes were worryingly intuitive.

'No.' Except for the ache in her heart, and the heat in her body, that said she wanted Luca Tebaldi—and that was a rocky road to nowhere. He only had to slant a look at her for her to know she was safer out of his way.

And she was making a really good job of that.

'I should find Maria,' she settled for, glancing around. 'We walked into town together, and I think she's with her friends.' She craned her neck, staring vaguely into the crowd.

'That's right,' Luca confirmed, resting one hard muscled forearm on the wall at the side of Jen's head. 'They're making the finishing touches to the floats for the parade. Didn't she tell you?'

He could hardly hide his satisfaction at catching her out, Jen noticed. 'I didn't know that. Thank you for telling me. I'll go and find her—'

He didn't move. Short of scrambling over him, there was no way past Luca. She was boxed in, in the doorway of a shop—and he was enjoying this. His dark eyes were amused. He liked having her exactly where he wanted her.

'No problem. I'll wait here,' she said with a shrug to show she couldn't care less. Leaning back against the door where she had a good view of the square, she settled in.

'I'm not happy leaving you here on your own. I have a duty of care—' Luca insisted.

'Since when?' she exclaimed.

'Since you came to work for me.'

'I work for your father,' Jen said coolly.

'It's all in the family,' Luca argued, his eyes firing at the thought of taking her on.

'And you always get your own way?' she said.

'Always,' he murmured. His black stare fixed on her lips.

As her heart went into overdrive, she moved around him. 'I'm going to find Maria—'

'No, you're not,' Luca said. 'You're going to dance with me.'

'Am I?'

'Yes, you are,' he murmured.

'But I don't dance,' she protested as he urged her out of the shadows in the direction of the dance floor. 'I've got two left feet *and* I'm wearing flip-flops.'

'So, kick them off,' Luca said as a space on the crowded floor miraculously appeared for them.

People were staring, and she didn't want to cause a scene. She gave Luca a frown, which only provoked him to raise a brow. Trying to remain immune to his machismo was hopeless, she concluded.

'Dance,' Luca commanded in a deep, husky voice.

'Was that an order? I don't see any hot coals,' she countered.

He laughed and pulled her into his arms.

It felt so good...dangerously good, and she wanted, longed, ached to have him kiss her again.

'Dance if you dare,' he challenged softly in her ear.

'Oh, I dare,' she said.

Curving one of his faint, heart-stopping smiles, Luca ordered softly, 'Prove it.'

'All right. I will,' she agreed, breaking free from his embrace.

'Dance as if you have no boundaries...'

'No problem,' she said. Raising her arms above her head, she began to move to the music.

His senses roared as Jen began to dance as if she was

dancing only for him. She stunned everyone into silence within the first few seconds, and not because she had suddenly become an expert, but because she oozed sensuality and showed no inhibition on the dance floor. The music gave her every excuse to use her body to the full, and she didn't hold back. She was hotter than hell, and every man knew it. She was with him, which they also knew.

At the back of his mind the same doubt remained. This woman could act many parts, and one of those parts was a girl who had caused his brother to leave her everything. More women joined in, and he was aware of their dark, flashing eyes seeking his approval, but he was only interested in Jen, who was a priestess of cool, surrounded by her acolytes. Her full hips undulated invitingly, while her nipples strained against the front of her dress. Kissing her was emblazoned on his mind. He could remember exactly how her lips had felt beneath his, and how warm and soft and smooth her skin had felt beneath his hands. Her eyes beneath the kitten mask glittered invitingly with wicked promise, but was she even aware of the stir she was causing? He thought not. She was far too absorbed in the dance.

As the music gradually increased in both pace and volume, the dancers moved towards a wild finale. Jen's sinuous dancing suggested she was available for pleasure, but her fierce, flashing eyes said not. It was a challenge he found irresistible.

She must be drunk on music and sunshine, Jen decided. She had never let herself go like this before. Conveniently, she blamed it on the feast day. Even her two left feet couldn't prevent her from enjoying herself.

'That's enough!'

She gasped as Luca dragged her close, and stared up at him, frowning. 'What's got into you?'

'I can't bear it,' he ground out, glaring at the other men.

Her vow to steer clear of him wasn't going so well, Jen concluded as she struggled to break free. It didn't help that she loved the pressure of his hard body against hers. 'What is your problem?' she demanded as Luca tightened his grip.

It was she who had the problem, Jen thought as Luca softened his grip and all she felt was regret. 'I want to dance *with* you,' he growled, keeping her rammed up hard against his body, where she could feel every inch of him in intimate detail. The thrust of his erection was all it took to blank her mind.

'I don't have a problem,' he murmured with his mouth so close to her ear it tingled. 'My only problem is you.'

She wanted him. She wanted this. She wanted to feel safe, close, and for his kisses and caresses to continue. She squeezed her eyes tightly shut, knowing it was wrong—dangerous—could lead to more heartbreak— what did she know about lovemaking?

'Don't fight me, Jen,' Luca murmured when she tried to pull away. 'You'll only lose—'

'Fight you?' If only she could win the battle of wills inside her and fight him to remain safe, emotionally safe.

'You'd better let me go,' she said, feeling her power to resist him fading into nothingness.

'Or else?' Luca murmured as he took off his mask.

'Or else I'll have to fight you every step of the way.'

'I look forward to it,' he said.

The look in his eyes sent heat rushing through her. And then the music changed, slowed, and grew sultry. The plangent melody wound a cord around Jen's heart, demanding she move in time with the music and with Luca.

As they began to sway together her hands seemed more sensitive as they rested on his chest. She could feel his heart beating beneath her fingertips, and it only took the smallest adjustment of her hands to bring her into contact with his naked skin. Once she'd touched him, she wanted to feel more of him—all of him, hot and hard against her—

No!

This was wrong. She had to shake herself out of the dream state. This was reality, not fantasy, and the danger of yielding to temptation could only lead to one place. Feeling her resistance, Luca released her. He stood staring down at her, his eyes full of questions.

Closing her eyes, she had to ask herself what she really wanted. The answer wasn't long in coming. 'Okay,' she said. 'Let's dance.'

CHAPTER NINE

SHE MIGHT HAVE two left feet, but she could dance with Luca. When he held her in his arms, her body responded perfectly, as if it knew exactly what to do. Luca moved so well he made it easy for her. He was fully in command, and that thought led her mind down all sorts of dark alleys where there were no boundaries. She had never been so acutely aware of her body, or its potential for pleasure. Luca had her in his erotic net, and she was a willing captive, safe behind her mask.

'Enough?' he murmured.

There's more? she thought.

Luca didn't speak. His hands remained on her arms, and then one hand slid down to her wrist. He linked their fingers, joining them. It was the most intimate thing she'd ever known as he led her away from the dance floor, steering her through the crowd. He took her across the square where the din of the festival roared in her ears, to a narrow, shaded street at the end of which was the sea. With every step Jen had the sense of leaving her safe world behind and entering somewhere exciting and new, and she was eager to embrace what felt like the next stage of her life.

With the town behind them, the ocean opened up in front of them. The part of Jen that had been so rigidly controlled for so long, knew it was time to stop before she got in any deeper. But how could anything wrong feel so right? she reasoned. There had been too much darkness, and when Luca glanced at her with his eyes full of warm amusement, she stared back to let him know how much she wanted this.

When they reached the cliff top, she issued a challenge. 'Race you down to the beach!'

'Too dangerous. I'd prefer you in one piece when we get there.'

With a laugh, she set off.

Reaching out, Luca caught hold of her. 'Slowly and carefully,' he instructed.

'Is that always your way? No. I didn't think so.' Pulling away from him, she ran off down the path. 'Here,' she said, stopping beside a moss-covered bank. Stretching out her arms, she threw back her head and closed her eyes. Luca came up behind her and wrapped his arms around her waist. It felt so right.

Jen's womanly curves yielding to his body moved him in every way there was. Physically, mentally and emotionally, he'd never felt anything like it. Her vital spirit was like a shot of adrenalin in his veins.

'Kiss me,' she demanded, staring up at him.

He needed no encouragement.

No. He needed sex. He was hungry for Jen. Holding her as they danced could never be enough. It had only stirred his senses until they roared.

'You have to kiss me,' she insisted. 'It's a special holiday.' Her eyes flashed a reckless message..

Pleasure anticipated was pleasure heightened, he concluded, bringing Jen down onto the bank beside him. He freed her hair, dropping kisses on her face and on the side of her neck as he did so, until he could lace his fin-

gers through its silky weight. 'Not enough?' he suggested
when she moved restlessly beneath him.

'What do you think?' she whispered against his mouth.

Her eyes were teasing him, but he could see Jen's vul-
nerability flickering behind her clear jade gaze.

'Touch me,' she said when he hesitated, and, taking
hold of his hand, she guided it to her breast.

'Like this?' he suggested, chafing one nipple very
gently between his forefinger and thumb.

'Oh, yes,' she gasped, clinging to him as he attended
to the other.

The sundress she was wearing might have been designed for love, with its tiny buttons from neck to waist.
He took his time opening them until only Jen's flimsy
white lace bra remained. Lifting her into his arms, he
carefully removed the dress, and then rested her back
on the ground, where she lay in an attitude of complete
trust with her arms above her head.

Running his fingertips very slowly down the length
of her body, he lingered on her breasts. He loved how
full they were, and how aroused she was. He moved on
over the curve of her belly and down to the soft, tempting swell of white lace. It was an area that merited his
full attention. She was beautifully plump, and he loved
the way her breathing quickened when he touched her.
He stroked her over the lace very lightly, and saw her
grab hold of hanks of seagrass in hands that had tightened into ivory fists.

Jen grabbed a hectic breath, wondering if she could
hold on much longer. She had never felt so aroused. It was
as if she were standing on a ledge, teetering, and longing
to fall off. She hadn't realised that her body was capable
of such levels of pleasure, and couldn't help herself edg-
ing her thighs just a little further apart.

Tugging his shirt over his head, Luca hunkered down on the bank at her side. Half naked, he was magnificent. Fully dressed, he was magnificent.

Fully naked?

She wasn't ready for that.

Luca shifted position until she had the perfect view of his thick, tangled hair, and the wide spread of his shoulders. His movements were unhurried and reassuring. She didn't even gasp when he eased her legs over his shoulders to suckle her through the heated white lace. But she whimpered, and that whimper became a cry of pleasure as she arced her body towards him in the hunt for more contact, more pressure. But Luca was too clever for her, and he moved again, to keep her waiting; deliberately, she thought.

'Please…' She writhed impatiently beneath him, but he left her frustrated as he stood to undo his belt and drop his jeans. He was totally unselfconscious. She heard his zipper go down and then heard him kick his jeans away. Burying her burning cheeks in her arms, she remained motionless as he came to kneel beside her.

'Are you shy?' he asked with a smile in his voice.

'No,' she said, raising her chin. This was the tipping point. This was the moment when she decided yes, or no.

Reaching out to him was all it took for Luca to bring her into his arms. It felt so good to be embraced by him. He felt so good; so strong, so big, so certain.

Leaning towards him, she brushed her lips against his. He unhooked her bra and tossed it away. Maintaining eye contact, he cradled her breasts. She couldn't stop herself exclaiming with pleasure, or rolling her head back, asking for more.

Weighing her breasts approvingly in his big, warm hands, he abraded the tip of each nipple very gently with his thumbnail, causing a wave of sensation to stream straight to her core. She was still pulsing with pleasure when he leaned forward to bury his head, before pulling back to suckle first one nipple and then the other, and when she thought sensation couldn't possibly increase, he dropped kisses on her neck, her ear lobes, and then her mouth. And that wasn't a teasing kiss, it was firm and deep as he continued to fondle her breasts. Lacing her fingers through his hair, she drew closer still, kissing him back, tongues tangling in the heat of discovery as Luca plundered her mouth.

He had not expected Jen to be quite so fiery. He had sensed the tiger in her, waiting to be unleashed, but she had wound her legs around him, and was rubbing her body against his with all the hunger of an experienced woman. She even gasped with relief when he stripped off her thong. She was impatient and he loved that. He loved the feel of her buttocks, so silky and soft and warm beneath his hands. He cupped them so he could bring her into direct contact with his straining erection. She cried out loud, a hungry, sobbing sound that prompted him to rotate his hips slowly.

'Please,' she begged him. 'Please...'

He replaced the pressure of his straining body with his hand. Using the slightly roughened pad of his forefinger, he explored and tested Jen's readiness. She was more than ready for him. She was hot and wet and swollen, and with each pass of his hand she rubbed herself against him in an attempt to increase the pressure of his touch.

'I think you need this,' he commented huskily.

'Oh, yes,' she gasped, exclaiming words of pleasure as he concentrated on the place where she needed him most.

'And this?' he said, upping the pace.

Her answer was a keening animal sound of need.

Clinging to him, eyes closed, her lips parted, she begged him in words that surprised him to stop teasing her. His answer was to ease a thigh between her legs and, lowering himself down, he caught just inside her. The pleasure of that, and the anticipation of yet more pleasure left her gasping for breath.

'Not yet,' he warned.

'Why not?' she demanded.

'Because waiting will only make it better for you.'

'I don't want to wait,' she assured him, moving restlessly.

'Then, I'll do the waiting for you.'

'Again?' He kissed her mouth as he stroked the tip of his erection back and forth, back and forth.

Closing her eyes, she sighed with pleasure. 'More,' she insisted, thrusting her hips towards him, but when he responded, she uttered a sharp cry.

'What aren't you telling me, Jen?'

'No! Don't stop now!'

But he had stopped, and he wouldn't continue until she explained.

'Nothing—honestly nothing,' she said. 'Cramp, that's all. I'm all right now.'

'Are you sure?'

'Of course I'm sure.' Her hands, her body and her smile gave him permission to continue. 'You're so big,' she exclaimed when he was on the brink of pulling back and, clutching his buttocks, she worked him in deeper.

'Relax,' he whispered when he was lodged to the hilt. 'Let me do all the work.'

'If you insist,' she whispered, smiling.

'I do insist.' He guessed it had been some time since Jen had made love, and however frantically she tried to urge him on he was equally determined to take things slowly. He brought his hand in to play up the levels of pleasure as she got used to him.

'Oh, yes...*yes*!' she exclaimed, moving in time with him to catch the full benefit of each firm stroke.

He clasped her buttocks, withdrew, and then sank deep, moving firmly and efficiently until she had no hope of holding on. 'Now,' he whispered on a note of command. She obeyed immediately and fell with a cry of shocked delight. She was lost for some time, bucking beneath him as he held her in place to receive the full benefit of each pulsing throb of pleasure, and when the storm had finally subsided and she asked for more, he laughed softly and brought her on top of him.

It was only a little deceit. Was it necessary to announce before she had her first proper sexual encounter that she was a virgin? Would Luca even care? She felt stupid at her age, anyway, admitting to something like that. There was no law that said you had to have sex by a certain age, and she'd always been so busy trying to set a good example to Lyddie that sex had kind of passed her by. And then she had convinced herself she could get by without it, and that it wasn't necessary to fill her life with all the angst and drama associated with an affair.

A little deceit was surely allowable under those circumstances. After all, what harm could it do?

CHAPTER TEN

JEN WAS STILL lying in Luca's arms when she remembered Maria would be waiting for her in the town. 'I should go back. Maria might be worried about me. Luca? Luca…?'

He was lying with his arm over his eyes, not trusting himself to look at Jen. He had thought that making love to her would ease the ache inside him, but instead it had only grown. He wanted her, and for more than just sex. He'd been starved of feelings—had starved himself of feelings—for far too long, and now he was overwhelmed by them.

Emotions hadn't troubled him since he was a boy. He'd learned to live without them after his mother died, and he had never let them in again. Why would he? His father didn't want them, and Raoul had decided to align himself with his father. Wanting Jen like this had never been part of his plan. It certainly wasn't part of his father's plan, and, however tenuous their relationship, Luca had never broken a promise to his father yet.

'I'll come with you,' he said as Jen reached for her clothes. 'There are dangers in town during this special holiday.'

'Worse than you?' she said. 'Seriously. I need to go. I don't want Maria to be worried about me.'

He reached for her and held her wrist. 'You'll stay with me tonight.'

'Will I?' she said. A smile crept onto her mouth as if she had tried to keep it away, but couldn't. 'You must be feeling very confident,' she said as she fastened her bra.

'I am,' he confirmed.

She laughed as he grabbed his clothes and tugged them on. He adjusted the straps on her sundress. She looked so beautiful. Flushed from their lovemaking with her hair in disarray and her lips red and swollen from his kisses, she somehow managed to look younger and more vulnerable than ever.

'So I'm to stay in the big house?' she said.

'That's the plan,' he confirmed.

Her cheeks pinked up like a child given a special treat. 'How old are you, Jen?'

'Old enough,' she said. 'Anyway, you should know— you must have studied my CV.'

'I have, but it didn't tell me how experienced you are.'

'Experienced enough,' she teased him.

'There were quite a few gaps in your résumé,' he recalled as questions started to grind away in his head.

'I'm twenty-four,' she said. 'Does that reassure you?'

Not really. She was very young.

'How old are you?' she demanded.

'Thirty-two.'

'Old Father Time.' She laughed as she ran her fingers through her hair to comb the grass strands out of it. 'But you're not married, and you don't have any children—so, seeing as we're playing the truth game, why's that, Luca?'

Could anything tempt him to bring a wife and children into the complicated world he inhabited? 'Don't let your imagination run riot,' he warned without answering her question.

'Why not?' she demanded, bundling her hair back up again. 'I'm sure you speculate about me.'

She was shrewd and covered her question in more smiles. Putting his hands on her shoulders, he turned her in the direction of the town. 'You need to be somewhere?' he reminded her.

She must have been intoxicated by the light mood that had sprung between them, and grabbed hold of his hands. 'So we have a future together?' she demanded, teasing him mercilessly.

'It will certainly extend into tonight,' he confirmed.

'Again, you're very confident, Signor Tebaldi.'

His mouth tugged in a half-smile. 'If you don't want to spend the night with me…'

Her blush gave her away. 'Unless I get a better offer,' she said, shooting him a provocative look.

He knew she was joking, but even the thought of another man looking at Jen was enough to stir his warrior genes. Sexually, she had been a revelation to him. She was fiery and passionate, but at the same time vulnerable. He had never found a woman like that. The closer he came to Jen, the more he could understand what his brother had seen in her—and even the thought of their friendship was enough to provoke a stab of jealousy inside him.

As soon as they were back in the town square Maria spotted them right away. Jen greeted his housekeeper with a hug. That suited him. The happier she was in Sicily, the more likely she was to stay. And he wanted her to stay, he realised, and for no other reason than he couldn't bear for her to go.

Shortly after Jen had found Maria, the friendly housekeeper left them to re-join her friends. Her first full day on the island had been incredible, Jen thought, smiling up at Luca. Being the sole focus of Luca's attention had been incredible. She would never forget the day when she made love with a hot Sicilian on a tiny island during a festival. If excitement never returned to her life again, she had that to cling on to.

She had more than that, Jen concluded as Luca turned to look at her. As his eyes locked with hers and they shared an intimate smile, she was ready to believe anything was possible. 'Tonight,' she whispered.

His faint smile set her heart racing. Then he turned away to speak to some people who had recognised him. She was a bystander, happily watching, when the elderly man leading the small family group reached for Luca's hand and kissed it.

'You are Don Tebaldi now,' he said in a loud, quavering voice that brought several murmurs of agreement from the crowd. 'Your father has earned his retirement. We look to you now, Luca.'

And then the man upon whom she had bestowed her long-preserved chastity patted the old man on the shoulder before drawing him close in an embrace to say, 'I will never let you down, Marco.'

There were tears in the old man's eyes by the time Luca released him. But even those tears, genuine though she knew they must be, couldn't make up for Jen's shock. She had managed to conveniently divorce Luca in her mind from his father, but now reality was staring her in the face.

She'd been so confident she could handle anything that she had walked willingly into a world she knew nothing about. How was she supposed to relax when everyone on the island treated Luca like a king? The elation of the day vanished, and was quickly replaced by concern.

'You two should dance,' the old man said, drawing Jen into the conversation with a warm smile. 'Go on,' he encouraged her. 'You have to dance for me now. My feet won't work!' He laughed with glee as he glanced around their little group, as if the warmth of his family and the protection of Luca made him happier than anything else on earth.

'What's wrong?' Luca asked, feeling Jen's tension as he brought her into his arms.

'Nothing,' she lied, smiling reassurance at the old man, who was watching them as he'd promised. Everything was wrong. Luca and Jen? The penniless student who'd had a thesis on right and wrong drummed into her by her mother, and the man who seemed to have inherited some sort of feudal fiefdom? How was that going to work? Just for a few fabulous hours, she had allowed herself to believe that it could.

'I don't believe you,' Luca said, drawing her close to stroke her hair. 'You're very tense.'

'Self-conscious,' she argued, which was true; there were a lot of people watching them. 'Don't worry, it's nothing,' she said as Luca wrapped his arms protectively around her.

'The parade's about to start,' he said as the music faded. Bringing his face close, he smiled into her eyes and kissed her.

'We shouldn't miss that,' she agreed, wishing she could lose the sense of an egg timer with the sand running out on their time of being as close as this.

She welcomed the distraction as Luca led her through the mass of people. She remembered Maria telling her to collect as many bead necklaces as she could when the parade passed, as they brought good luck.

She needed a barrel full, Jen mused ruefully. She had

to stop wanting things she couldn't have, she thought, glancing at Luca.

They hadn't even reached the main street when Luca drew to a halt, and pulled her into a shaded alleyway. 'Why?' she whispered.

'Because I want you?' he said with shrug.

He kissed her, and then he kissed her again, until finally she softened in his arms. 'We can't!' Jen protested in a voice trembling with excitement.

'Why not?' Luca murmured, caressing her tenderly as he spoke.

'Because we're in public?'

'And the beach is different?'

'The beach was deserted,' she reminded him.

'And so is this passageway. Where's your sense of adventure, Jen?'

Luca's smile was irresistible. His touch was too. And he was right in that ancient buildings rose high on either side of them, throwing the narrow cut-through into deep shadow. Reaching up, she wound her arms around his neck.

He kept on kissing her as he pressed her against the wall. His body blocked out all the light, leaving nothing but him and sensation, and as his hands began to work their magic she knew there was no more talking to be done. There was only touching and feeling, and whispering to each other as they exchanged increasingly heated kisses. She ached for him, and when he reached beneath her dress to strip off her thong, she let him lift her so she could wrap her legs around his waist.

The touch of Jen's tiny hand gripping him, nursing him, was an incendiary device to his senses. 'Now,' she begged him, thrusting her hips fiercely towards his.

They both needed this. She cried out with relief when

he thrust deep. He took her in one firm stroke while she grasped his biceps with fingers that had turned to steel as she worked her hips strongly with his. They both felt the same urgency, and it didn't allow for finesse. Jen's control soon shattered, as did his shortly after. The noise of the crowd drowned out her release.

'No one can hear you,' he reassured her, stroking her to soothe her as she slowly came down. Her eyes were still black with arousal as she stared into his face. He couldn't let that pass, and started to move again.

'I love that you're so intuitive,' she gasped against his neck, groaning in time with each thrust as he took her firmly.

'Relax,' he whispered. 'Do nothing, Concentrate.'

'Do nothing. Concentrate… On?'

'Sensation,' he suggested, moving steadily to please her.

She laughed softly in between appreciative groans. 'Is there anything else?'

When Jen was finally able to express her approval with a deep satisfied sigh, he kissed her. 'I think you're going to be taking up quite a lot of my time;'

'I hope so,' she said as he carefully lowered her to her feet. Her eyes cleared and just for a moment she seemed so innocent. He wanted to forget that there could be any doubt about that. But he couldn't. Not yet. It frustrated him to think that he knew her so intimately, and yet he didn't really know Jen at all.

'Beads,' she reminded him.

'Whatever you wish.' As they smiled into each other's eyes, there was just a moment when he believed they could be like any other couple.

He led her out of the alley, back into the heat and glaring light of the main event. He waved to one of the passing floats and was rewarded with an armful of gaudy necklaces.

'Are these all for me?' Jen demanded as he draped them around her neck. 'You have to wear one too,' she insisted.

'What do you think?' she asked, standing back to check him out, once she had looped the necklace over his head.

'I think it's a great look,' he joked, wondering when he'd enjoyed himself more.

'I agree. Day-Glo pink is definitely your colour,' she said as he made her a mock bow.

His heart banged in his chest. This was getting really complicated, and it was only day one.

Jen hadn't realised that Luca was due to crown the Queen of the festival. But, of course, it made perfect sense. As the uncrowned king of the island, who better for the task?

'I'll stay in the crowd and watch, if you don't mind?' she said when Luca wanted her to join him on the stage. 'I can feel the atmosphere better down here,' she explained.

'Being jostled by the crowd?' he asked, frowning.

'I'm sure I'll survive it.'

'Be sure you do,' Luca said as he leaned in to kiss her lingeringly on the mouth.

She had to be realistic about this, Jen's sensible side warned as she watched Luca mount the stage. This thing between them had happened quickly, and it could fade just as quickly. But her sensible side didn't stand a chance, because her heart was fully committed to the dangerous path she was taking.

She wasn't alone in her admiration for Luca. The excitement in the crowd was almost hysterical when he appeared on stage. Even dressed casually, he was magnificent. Just like a king, she thought, though he had the popular touch too. Luca had a quiet confidence that said he could deal with any problem and would do so efficiently and permanently. It was to be hoped she never became a problem for him, Jen thought, growing tense. She had more sense, she told herself firmly. She'd know when it was time to pull back. Unfortunately, all her body was interested in, was when they would make love again.

She'd never met anyone like Luca Tebaldi before, Jen reasoned as Luca addressed the crowd.

Was this love at first sight?

More like being swept up in a whirlwind, she concluded.

Was that how it felt to be in love?

Was it possible to fall in love with someone in such a short time?

Why not, if it was right? Jen concluded. Some friendships and love affairs took years to develop, while others sprang from the heart fully formed.

Her heart raced as Luca glanced down from the stage to smile at her. Even if he didn't return her feelings, it wouldn't change what she felt for him. It was thanks to him that she'd had the chance to experience the most wonderful feeling in the world, and she was in no hurry to let go of it.

CHAPTER ELEVEN

'YOU SEEM PREOCCUPIED,' Luca commented as the crowd began to drift away from the stage. 'Is there a problem?'

He was the problem. Her mixed-up feelings for Luca were the problem. Since the day Luca had arrived at the casino her world had been turned upside down, and it hadn't stopped spinning since.

Perhaps they could talk—really talk and open up to each other if they left now. Her feelings for Luca were out of control—and not just because of the amazing sex. He was different in Sicily, more relaxed than in London, and now she knew why. This island was his home, his kingdom, his birthright, and she wasn't sure what that entailed. She'd only experienced life within certain boundaries, and had taken a great leap over them. It would be sensible to get things back on a professional footing, Jen concluded. That would probably be a relief for Luca too.

'Will I see the jewels tomorrow?' she asked as they walked back to the house.

'Why not tonight?' Luca offered. 'Why not now,?'

'If you're sure?' Her heart started thumping for a very different reason.

Don Tebaldi's secret hoard of priceless jewels was discussed with awe across the world of fine jewellery, but no one had ever seen the gems in one place before. Ru-

mours abounded, as many were cursed, and all of them
had a bloody history. Which brought Jen's thinking back
to the so-called curse on the Emperor's Diamond, the
precious gem that would be the centre of her exhibition.
She didn't believe an inanimate object could carry any
sort of power. She wasn't superstitious—or she hadn't
been, up to now.

You had to have something really big at risk before
you could believe in things like that, she thought as a
prescient shiver tracked down her spine.

Back at the big house, Luca took her straight upstairs.
He opened a bedroom door and stood back. 'After you,'
he said.

Jen hovered uncertainly on the threshold. The blinds
were drawn, the room was dark, and the air smelled stale
and musty. 'Is your father's collection in here?' she asked,
frowning.

He waited until Jen was inside the room before explaining that a new vault was under construction now he
was in charge, but until that was ready his father's hoard
remained, quite literally, under the bed.

'I'm fascinated,' Jen admitted. 'I can't wait to see
them.'

She had imagined some wonderful state-of-the-art cel-
lar, with air-con and doors that slid silently closed, complete with complicated locking systems, but Luca simply
put his shoulder to the mahogany frame, and moved the
bed to reveal a trapdoor. Shooting the bolts, he opened
the structure on its creaking hinges.

Jen guessed her face must have been a picture. 'Down
there?' she exclaimed as he indicated a ladder.

'I hope you don't have a nervous disposition?' he
mocked lightly.

'I've been alone with you,' she said, clinging to humour. 'I'm neither claustrophobic, nor afraid of the dark,' she assured him when Luca gave her one of his ironic looks.

'Good, because it's deep and dark and dank, and there may be spiders,' he countered, laughing when she shuddered. 'I did warn you that my father is one of the world's last true eccentrics, didn't I?'

Jen shrugged. 'Maybe. Do your worst,' she challenged.

'Take care as you come down the ladder,' Luca warned, turning serious.

He was waiting to steady her at the bottom as she took in her surroundings. They were standing in a small box-like room, with a reinforced steel door at one end. Spinning the combination, Luca opened the door and switched on the light inside. She could see now that the walls were lined with stacks of jewellery boxes, large and small, and there were some hessian sacks resting against the wall.

'This is it?' she said with surprise.

'This is it,' Luca confirmed. 'My father was a hoarder and nothing pleased him more than to dip his hand into one of those sacks and feel the priceless jewels running through his fingers.'

'They're just loose in there?' She couldn't believe it, especially when she remembered the neat displays in the vault at Smithers & Worseley.

'And all jumbled up,' Luca confirmed. 'Now can you see why we need you to sort things out? I'll bring them up,' he offered.

Whatever she had expected, it wasn't this, Jen thought as Luca upended the first sack on top of his father's bed. 'How many sacks are there down there?' she managed in a voice that barely made it above a squeak.

'Half a dozen or so.'

She stared down in amazement at his father's haul.

Even in the gloom of the bedroom they seemed to sparkle with a feverish light.

'Are they all cursed?' she asked faintly.

'I thought you didn't believe in that?'

'I don't,' she said with far less certainty than she had before.

'They can't hurt you. Only life and people can do that.'

'I know,' she agreed. 'It's just that I've never seen so many valuable gemstones lumped together like this. I can't even imagine their combined value, or how long it's going to take me to identify each one—did your father keep any records?'

'I doubt it.'

'This is going to take longer than I expected.'

'Around six months?' Luca suggested.

'I didn't imagine I'd be here so long.'

'But you've finished your college course?'

'Yes, I have, but still...'

'I'll get you all the help you need. I doubt my father even looked at these gems more than once before he tossed them into the sacks.'

Like penny sweets, Jen thought, refusing to think about value, or the good that could be done with such a sum. 'This collection is unique.'

'And you must be eager to start work?'

'I am,' she confirmed, but as she stared into Luca's eyes, she wondered how she would bear to be on the island if he distanced himself.

Get over it, Jen told herself firmly. She was here to do a job, though she couldn't deny that the amount of jewels to be catalogued and displayed had shocked her.

'A summer in Sicily,' Luca said in an attempt to lighten the atmosphere, she guessed. 'What's so bad about that? What would you do if you weren't here on the island—

work in the club, and at the auction house? Why do that when you can be here enjoying a paid holiday?'

'Hardly that,' she said, glancing at the mountain of jewels.

'You can do the work you love at your own pace., And living here has to be better than living in a bedsit?'

She couldn't argue with that, so why didn't she feel good about this? Why was there still something nagging at the back of her mind? She should be thrilled. Luca was right. This was a wonderful opportunity.

But not once had he mentioned them spending time together, Jen realised, and, though she hated herself for the weakness, she couldn't help wondering if, once she got to work, she would see him again.

Reassurance was needed, Luca concluded as he took a shower. He'd got it in hand. Jen had been thrown by the extent of his father's collection, and more especially by the realisation that it would take her months, rather than days or weeks, to complete the work she had been engaged to do. He had left her at the gate of the guest house to give her some time to get used to the idea. If she pulled out now it would put an end to his investigations and that wasn't going to happen. He had suggested dinner at the big house with him and, after a few moments of contemplation, she'd agreed.

He pulled on his jeans and snapped his belt through the loops. He parked the shave. It could wait until morning. He was impatient to see her again. He glanced in the mirror. Running his fingers through his hair had only succeeded in making it more unruly. His eyes beneath upswept brows glittered darkly.

Because he wanted Jen.

And that couldn't wait until the morning.

She was waiting for him in the library, leafing through one of his favourite books, when he came downstairs. She looked exquisite with her red-gold hair cascading down her back in a waterfall of waves, and with her apparently innocent, make-up-free face. The power of her beauty shocked him. He was transfixed and stopped just inside the door to take her in. She had picked one of the dresses from her new collection, a simple shift in aquamarine silk; a colour that framed her fiery Celtic looks to perfection. The dress was knee-length, and moulded her shapely figure with loving attention to detail.

'*Master and Commander*?' she commented, breaking the spell as she replaced the book on the shelf.

'That's my Sunday name.'

'The book,' she countered with an amused look. 'I love your library. You're a very lucky man.'

'I love it too,' he said as he crossed the room to join her. 'It was here that I learned the Emperor's Diamond was said to be the most significant stone in Emperor Napoleon's coronation crown—hence the curse. Napoleon's life didn't exactly end on a high point, as I'm sure you know?' He smiled and shrugged. 'I've always been fascinated by the Napoleonic wars.'

'Are you sure it isn't the tactics of warfare that fascinate you?' she challenged, and within seconds they were back to verbal jousting.

'Can we agree to lay aside our weapons for one night?' he suggested.

'In the interest of…?'

'Getting to know each other better?'

'I thought we already did that?' Her mouth slanted in a teasing line.

He pointed to one of the sofas.

Raising a brow at the implied instruction, she moved to put the library table between them.

'Battle tactics?' he suggested.

'Common sense avoidance tactics,' she countered.

'I hope you haven't been put off by the scale of the work here?'

'Do I look overwhelmed?'

No. She looked beautiful. 'Please…sit down…'

'Is that an invitation or an instruction?'

He shrugged. 'It's a suggestion you can take up or not.'

'What do you want to know about Raoul?' she said as she sat down.

She caught him by surprise. 'Are you a mind reader?'

'I use a crystal ball,' she assured him dryly. 'Seriously? I'd want to know, if I were you.'

'You're right,' he confirmed. 'Anything you can tell me about my brother—everything you can remember,' he said.

'I might not be able to tell you everything.'

'What do you mean?' he asked.

'Just that.' Her emerald-green eyes held his stare steadily.

'Am I being unreasonable?' he suggested.

'No.' But her lips had tightened as if Jen had to be careful what she said. 'I'll tell you what I can,' she confirmed. 'But only on one condition.'

'And that is?'

'You have to answer my questions too.'

'It's a deal,' he agreed, coming to sit across from her with a low table in between them. 'Let's start with how well you knew Raoul.'

'I didn't sleep with him, if that's what you mean.'

'I'm not asking if you slept with him. I'm asking you how well you knew him.'

'Hardly at all,' she admitted.

Which didn't make sense. Either she was lying through her teeth, or Raoul had suffered some form of brainstorm that had prompted him to act so rashly in her favour.

'It's my turn to ask the next question,' she said when he was about to press her on this point.

He sat back and indicated that she should get on with it, while he mulled over the question of whether it was possible to trust a woman who had just told him that she hardly knew his brother when Raoul had left her a fortune with no strings attached.

'Is your business legitimate, Luca?'

That was quite an interesting start to her line of questioning. 'Of course it's legitimate.' He prided himself on the absolute legitimacy of every one of his business dealings. 'What are you implying?'

'I'm just curious,' she admitted. 'The people here hold you in such high esteem.'

'Is that so wrong?'

'They kiss your hand as if you ruled over them.'

'I love them,' he said simply. 'My family has protected this island for generations. If you're asking if the islanders regard me as some sort of king, then, no, of course they don't. They come to me for advice, as they came to my father before me, and my grandfather before that. If I can help them, I will. And that's it,' he assured her. 'And now it's my turn to ask the question. How long have you known my brother?'

'Since I started working at the club. He was a regular there—but you know that. Raoul was always lovely to chat to—always so pleasant and polite.'

'And that's it?' he pressed.

'I don't know what you're getting at. Raoul talked about you and I talked about Lyddie. We got sad together.

It was my job to cheer him up. Not just my job, my pleasure,' she said thoughtfully. 'Raoul was different.'

'How was he different?'

'Special. Raoul was special. He didn't come to the casino to wallow in self-pity, he came to forget, which was why he played the tables every night.'

'Forget,' Luca murmured.

Guilt had struck him again at the thought that Raoul might have wanted to change his life, but Luca hadn't been there to help him. Raoul had tried so hard to win their father's love, and had failed as utterly as he had. The thought that Raoul had had no one but this girl to confide in cut him like a knife.

'You were kind to Raoul,' he said, staring keenly at her.

'Of course I was kind to Raoul. Your brother was kind to me. We always made time for each other…' Her voice tailed away as if she wished that she could have done more for Raoul too.

'And there was definitely nothing more between you than friendship?'

'What could it be? Blackmail? Sex? Stop it,' she insisted. 'There was nothing between your brother and me, but friendship. It doesn't always have to be about sex.'

'It usually is between a man and a woman.'

'Well, not this time,' she assured him hotly. 'And if all these ugly thoughts have been swirling round in your head, how could you make love to me? Was it a test, Luca? Has this all been some sort of horrible game?'

As she sprang to her feet he caught hold of her, and, dragging her close, he assured her, 'This is not a game, Jen. This is all too real for me.'

'And to me,' she assured him tensely. 'Do you think I like being interrogated as if I've got something to hide?'

'I think that if I had known your sister, and you met me and asked me about Lyddie, I would tell you every tiny detail I could remember. Nothing you can tell me about Raoul is too small or inconsequential. Everything you know about Raoul will colour in the picture that was my brother—my estranged brother. I need this information like I need air to breathe, and for no other reason than I loved my brother, and now it's too late to tell Raoul just how much he meant to me.'

CHAPTER TWELVE

HIS LOVE FOR his brother was stronger than his need to know why the woman in front of him would inherit Raoul's estate, Luca realised. Every word he'd said to Jen was true. He was desperate for the smallest detail, and if there was something Jen wasn't telling him—all his demons launched themselves on him at once. 'There has to be something more to your friendship with Raoul—something you're not telling me.'

'Why?' Jen demanded. 'Why do you think I'm hiding something? Why does there have to be more than the truth?'

'Because there must be,' he insisted. 'You have to be hiding something. Maybe it's a secret my brother couldn't bring himself to tell anyone but you— I don't know,' he admitted with frustration. He was so used to being in control, this level of emotional incontinence was new to him, and he had to take a moment to calm down.

'You answer my question,' Jen insisted.

Silence.

'What is your business here on the island? You haven't told me yet, and I need to know exactly what I'm involved in.'

'My life on the island isn't connected to my business, if that helps. I don't know what else to tell you, other than the fact that your job remains the same. You've been hired to catalogue jewels for a sick old man, and then set up an exhibition that he can be proud of. I want his life to end well, and you can supply that ending for him. All you need to know about me is that everything I do is within the law, and that nothing I do could ever hurt you, *or* Raoul's memory. My business interests extend across the world, and, though they are many and varied, *all* of them are legitimate.'

'So why couldn't you find time for your brother, if your business is so vast and you have so many people working for you?'

'It was the other way around, Jen. Raoul didn't want to see me.'

'Because you couldn't accept him—' She had stopped as if she'd said too much.

'Accept him?' he pressed urgently. 'Accept his gambling debts, do you mean?'

Jen looked increasingly uncomfortable, but remained stubbornly silent.

'Tell me,' he insisted. 'Why can't you tell me what you know about Raoul? I wouldn't be this cruel to you, if our situations were reversed.'

'I made a promise,' she fired back. 'And I won't break that promise. I can say this—it wasn't easy for Raoul to live in his father's world. I think he came to believe that it wasn't even possible.'

'Well, I can understand that,' he agreed grimly, 'but it still doesn't explain why Raoul felt it necessary to distance himself from me.'

'He believed you'd grown apart and he didn't know how to heal the gulf.'

'Clearly,' he murmured bitterly. 'But I think you know

exactly what the problem was, but you choose not to tell me.'

She shrugged. 'It's only the same as you refusing to spell out what you do.'

'I'm in the security business, as you know.'

'And that's it?' she queried, looking sceptical.

'That's it,' he confirmed. 'If I go into any more detail my business will no longer be secure. I can tell you that my operatives protect some of the most high-profile people in the world, and also provide safe escort for some of the most valuable items on the planet.'

'Like the Emperor's Diamond.'

'Exactly,' he confirmed.

'You said your father's retired to Florida, so who's going to take over his business interests?'

'No one. What remains of his empire has been dismantled.'

'By you?'

'It's enough for you to know that I will never take over my father's business—not in the way you think, though I do have a lifelong responsibility towards the people on this island.'

'What about the old man who kissed your hand?'

'Traditions take a long time to change, and the older men and women on the island don't know how things will turn out now my father's left the island. It's up to me to reassure them, and that will take a little time.'

'I appreciate your honesty,' she said after a few moments.

'As I would appreciate yours,' he said pointedly. 'Who else can I ask about Raoul?'

'I'll tell you everything that doesn't break my promise to your brother.'

Jen was in a bind. She wanted to be completely open

with Luca, but Raoul had begged her not to share some of the things he'd told her. It would break his father's heart, he'd said. Like Luca, Raoul had only ever felt concern for the father who had shunned him and who had never shown him any love.

Why did people like Don Tebaldi have children in the first place? His two sons had cared for him more than he'd ever cared for them. Jen's eyes stung with tears as she remembered the highly charged conversations she'd shared with Raoul. He'd been such a kind and funny man, in spite of the lack of love in his life. Raoul had felt things deeply, and now he was dead.

'Please,' Luca said quietly.

She couldn't help but think of Lyddie, and how hungry Jen would be for the smallest nugget of information. 'You mustn't blame yourself,' she said.

'Tell me, and then I'll decide.'

'All right, I will.' She paused. 'Raoul was gay, and he didn't think you would understand.'

Luca was quiet for the longest time. 'What?' he said at last, staring at her in disbelief.

'Raoul was gay,' Jen repeated. 'Once he came out, he said it would be impossible for him to come back to Sicily to face you and his father.'

'He couldn't face me?' Luca repeated. 'Raoul was gay? Is that…everything?'

'Yes.'

'That's what stopped him getting in touch with me? Are you sure?'

Burying his head in his hands, Luca squeezed his arms together, as if the hurt inside him had to be held in.

Lifting his head, he stared at her with incomprehension. 'My brother couldn't tell me that he was gay?' And then, quietly, 'Am I such a monster?'

'No, Luca. No—'

'How did he think I'd react? Raoul was my brother. I loved him unconditionally. Don't tell me that that's what made him gamble? No. *No*—'

'Luca, please...'

Coming around the library table, she reached for him, but he pulled away.

'My love for Raoul was absolute, unquestioned. I only ever wanted him to be happy. What went wrong?' he asked softly.

'He loved you,' Jen said with confidence. 'Raoul couldn't bear the thought of losing your love.'

'He could never lose my love,' Luca exclaimed fiercely.

'But what about your father?'

Luca made an angry dismissive sound.

'And the islanders?'

He shook his head firmly at this. 'There are no people on this earth more loving and accepting than the people who share our island home.'

'Then, it must be your father who stopped Raoul coming back. I got the sense during some of our conversations that Raoul had tested the waters and found them deeply unwelcoming.'

'There was a conversation between me and my father at Raoul's funeral,' Luca remembered, narrowing his eyes as he thought back. 'I didn't think anything of it at the time.'

'And now?'

'And now I know I'm a fool, because I should have protected Raoul better than I did. I should have been there for him when he needed me. I wish he'd trusted me enough. I'll never be able to make it up to him now—'

Hurt was bleeding from him as surely as if he'd been shot. She reached out. 'Blaming yourself won't help, Luca.'

'But *Dio!* It hurts.' Balling his hands into fists, he rested them on the library table, with his head down, grimacing as if a real physical pain had gripped him. 'You have no idea how much it hurts.'

'But I do,' Jen said gently, 'because I hurt too. There are always things left unsaid, and things we wished we'd had time to say, or do, when someone we love dies, but that doesn't mean you didn't love Raoul enough, or I didn't love Lyddie enough. It just means that life can be cruel sometimes, taking those we love without warning.'

When Lyddie died there were so many things left unsaid. How much worse must it have been for Luca who had been estranged from his brother before Raoul's death? Both the brothers were the losers in this. Their father didn't have the capacity to love anything apart from his secret hoard of jewels, it seemed to Jen. She felt sorry for Don Tebaldi, for the love he'd wasted.

'Are you sure you've told me everything?' Luca demanded, searching her face.

'Not everything, no,' Jen admitted. 'But I've told you everything I can without breaking my pledge to your brother. I can tell you this. It wouldn't help you to know anything more, so why don't you let Raoul's secrets die with him?'

'I can't do that.' Luca's voice had gained a hard edge. 'And I don't appreciate you deciding what you will and won't tell me.'

'It's up to me what I tell you,' Jen said without rancour, making allowances for how upset he was.

'Why?' Luca demanded, his expression blackening.

'Because I'm protecting the living as well as the dead.'

'And what do you mean by that?'

'That's all I'm prepared to say.' She would keep her word to his brother. 'I promised Raoul that if I ever got the chance to meet you, I would tell you as much as I have. I begged him to get in touch with you. I told him that if you were anything like him, all you'd care about was Raoul's happiness.'

'You were right to do that, and I tried, but Raoul always kept me at arm's length, which was why we drifted apart.'

'Perhaps you were both partially responsible,' Jen suggested.

Luca shook his head. 'I can't answer that,' he said grimly, 'but there are things I have to know.'

'What things?' Jen demanded tensely, flinching away from the harsh expression on his face, which seemed to be directed at her. 'You're talking in riddles, and I've already told you that I can't help you any more than I have.'

'You must—'

'No,' she said firmly. 'I can't.'

In his frustration at her refusal, Luca grabbed hold of her. She was acutely aware of every inch of him pressed up hard against her curves, but making love in anger was impossible for her, and she told him so.

He stared at her in a fury of grief, and then groaned. 'Forgive me. This is not the way it's supposed to be. I loved Raoul so much, and now he's gone, and if I'm not careful, I'll drive you away.' His face softened as Jen inhaled sharply with surprise. 'And then who will catalogue my father's collection?' he teased.

Jen slowly shook her head. 'You're impossible.'

'I do my best,' Luca agreed with a wry tug of his mouth.

It took her a few moments to relax completely and accept that, just as she could be overwhelmed by her long-neglected emotions, so could Luca.

'Forgive me,' he murmured.

Things changed rapidly when Luca took her in his arms. The anger between them subsided and another emotion altogether filled the gap. She was acutely aware of the insistent thrust of Luca's thick erection, and the very last thing she wanted to do was to argue with him. The moment he kissed her, she knew she was lost. She returned his hunger with matching heat. All she could think about was claiming him and reliving the pleasure they'd so recently shared. Whatever they'd said, and whatever accusations had flown between them, there was only one imperative now, and that was to be one with Luca.

Their tongues tangled. Her fingers bit into his shoulders. She ground her body against him, seeking more contact, but it could never be enough. She needed to be one with him, hot flesh to hot flesh, and, groaning with need, she clasped his buttocks to bind him tight to her.

Wordless sounds of need accompanied her actions as she released him to work on his belt buckle. She had it free in a couple of seconds. Next she tackled the button at the top of his zipper. Her hands were shaking as she fumbled to push it through the mean little hole, but to her relief his zip came down smoothly. Her first sight of his erection was her reward. Clearly visible through his black silk shorts, it was a prize she was determined to lose no time claiming. Cupping him in her hands, she sank to her knees. Freeing him from his shorts, she took him deep into her mouth. Working him, she had the satisfaction of hearing Luca groan. Tangling his hands in her hair, he cupped her head to keep her close. For every pass she made, and every groan he gave, she was also becoming increasingly aroused, but her greedy body would have to wait, because this was all for him.

'Yes,' Luca ground out on a stifled breath.

She teased him mercilessly with her tongue, before increasing the suction and taking him deep again.

'Enough!' he exclaimed. 'Or you'll be so frustrated, you'll never come down—'

'I'll risk it for you,' she said recklessly.

Luca disagreed, and sweeping her into his arms, he arranged her to his liking on the firm seat of the Chesterfield. Bringing her skirt to her waist, he exposed her flimsy thong.

He had placed her over the sidearm of the sofa so her upper body was stretched out on the seat and she could see everything he was doing to her. That was his intention, she was sure. The thought alone was enough to excite her. She had never imagined that anything could be as arousing as this. Her hips were lifted high on the padded arm when Luca nudged his way between her thighs. He stared down at her, his face, so full of the promise of pleasure to come. She cried out on a shaking breath as he slowly drew the smooth dome of his erection down the length of the infuriating barrier that was her thong. Throwing her head back, she closed her eyes to concentrate on the ache of pleasure. Hungry for more, she arced her hips in an attempt to catch more contact. With a sound of denial, Luca pulled back. Reaching down, he cupped her. The warmth of his hand, and the knowledge that those skilful fingers were so close to doing what she needed them to do, was a rocket to her senses. She thrashed her head about as he allowed her a couple of passes, and gasped noisily with excitement when he lifted her to dispose of her thong. Having done this, he spread her legs wide. She was completely exposed, completely at his mercy.

'Please,' she begged.

'Do you need this?' Luca enquired in a gentle, seemingly concerned tone.

'You know I do,' she gasped as he fisted his erection.

He laughed softly as he ran the tip across her heated flesh, making her whimper from the extremes of pleasure. And he did this not once, but several times. The sensation was exquisite torture. She never wanted it to end, and, desperate for more, she lifted her hips, hoping to catch more of him, but he always moved away in time. She thrust her hips again, and this time almost caught him. She wouldn't trust to luck next time. Capturing his buttocks in her hands, she bound his hips to hers, and, with a deep groan of surrender, Luca plunged deep.

'Oh, yes…yes…' This was what she wanted…this was what she needed. Working fast and hard, she moved with him, and moments later fell.

'More?' Luca murmured when she was quiet again.

She laughed contentedly. It was the only answer he needed. Her body was still pulsing with pleasure when he plunged deep again. Hard and flexing, he was as hungry for this as she was. Reaching up, she invited herself into his arms. Lifting her, he held her securely as she wrapped her legs around his waist. On a joint breath of noisy approval, he thrust up and into her, hard and deep. This time it was an even wilder dance towards release. They were both fierce. She couldn't get enough of him, and it seemed Luca felt the same. She had to have him…*this*!

'Now!' she exclaimed, unable to wait a moment longer.

They plunged together, shuddering and convulsing, helpless in the grip of pleasure so extreme they could only cry out repeatedly as the giant waves of sensation battered them relentlessly. She was weak and shaking by the time it eased off, and then Luca suggested huskily, 'Bed?'

'Will we even make it that far?' she teased him groggily.

'Once more against the door?' he suggested. 'Just to take the edge off?'

'Anywhere you like,' she agreed. 'But the door is too far away.'

He laughed softly. 'Bed,' Luca decreed. 'I need a firm surface and time to enjoy you.'

'You're not doing that already?' Jen protested. It was her turn to laugh. 'You think you're going to win this, don't you?' she said. Luca was still inside her, and she was an able student.

'Witch,' he accused as she tightened her inner muscles around him.

'Door,' she instructed.

CHAPTER THIRTEEN

JEN SITTING CROSS-LEGGED on the bed feeding him with pizza was definitely a first. Pizza was the only thing they could find in the freezer, but it was Jen who was the revelation. Six months didn't seem nearly long enough to spend together now. He could never have imagined this when he had first come up with his plan, he reflected as they sat facing each other naked, wolfing down food to keep up their strength.

'What are you thinking?' she pressed him when he stared at her.

'First off—I never imagined collecting my auction lot quite like this. And don't worry,' he assured her. 'I think it's a great improvement on a quiet supper at the club.'

She laughed. 'I should hope so. And what else?'

'Things you don't need to know.' Like, incredibly for him, he was wishing they could be a normal couple without secrets and a fair chance of seeing where this might lead. 'Crazy thoughts,' he admitted when Jen gave him one of her shrewd looks.

'Like?' she mumbled, cramming another triangle of crisp dough into her mouth.

Her eyes pinned him, demanding the truth, but it was a truth he couldn't give her without losing what they had. But to get her to tell him more, he had to give her something. 'The last I heard from Raoul, he was talking about building a camp for kids here on the island—kids like him, he said. I didn't know what he meant at the time, but maybe it makes sense now. What?' he prompted when Jen frowned.

It was Jen's turn to mask her thoughts, and he was instantly suspicious. He must have hit on something close to the secret she was keeping for Raoul.

Moving the pizza plate away, he brought her into his arms to ask, 'Did Raoul ever mention the idea of a summer camp to you?'

'Hmm.' Jen sighed with contentment as she snuggled deeper into his arms. She rubbed her cheek against his chest like a sleepy kitten. Anything to distract him, he thought.

'We should make the most of this,' she told him softly. 'I start work tomorrow, and I'm pretty obsessive when I'm working. I'll be like a mole underground, only surfacing briefly and even then I'll be distracted. And it will take me months to finish the assignment,' she added, turning her face up to look at him.

'Six months,' he repeated, staring away into the middle distance.

'Well, that's what you said,' she reminded him with a wry quirk of her mouth. 'I'll have to see if I can work faster.'

'Are you so eager to leave?' Her answer was suddenly very important to him.

She shrugged as she smiled and huffed. 'I'm sure you'll be pleased to see the back of me.'

She obviously knew something he didn't.

Jen woke the next morning and turned to find Luca waiting to make love to her.

They kissed long and slow. 'I was wondering how long it would take you to wake up,' he said.

'You could have started without me.'

He laughed softly, deep in his chest.

'My body works just fine on automatic,' she whispered.

'Let's test that, shall we?' he suggested.

His body moved firmly and slowly to please hers, as she gradually made the transition from sleep and dreaming about making love with Luca, to discovering that the actual fact was so much better.

'Good morning,' he murmured as she began to move with more intent.

He moved behind her, while she curled up, giving him all the access he needed. Accentuating the angle of her body, she offered him more. She offered him everything. Drunk on pleasure, she decided she could happily stay in bed all day—that was, if she didn't have work to do. But she was so very sensitive after so much concentrated and skilful attention from Luca that it took very little to bring her to the brink. Holding her in place as she bucked frantically, he was flattered and not a little surprised.

'That was sudden,' he murmured, smiling against her mouth.

'I can't always wait for your command,' she told him before teasing the seam of his lips with her tongue. 'And it's your turn now,' she insisted, turning to face him.

Goodness knew where all this confidence had come from, Jen thought as she straddled Luca. It could only have come from Luca. He was such a generous lover he made it obligatory to respond. And he was so gorgeous that her heart squeezed tight just at the sight of him. Sweeping ebony brows over those knowing black eyes, and that mouth... Leaning forward, she brushed her lips against his and felt his arms close around her. She pressed into him until there was nothing between them, and they were one.

'You are the best,' she whispered, pulling back to look at him. 'The absolute best.' That was the closest she could come to admitting that she loved him. And she did love him. She had loved Luca practically from the first moment they met. It made no sense then, and it made no sense now, but it was a fact. Her heart was full when she was with him. Her body was his. His body was hers. Leaving money and position in life aside, they were equally matched in so many things. This just felt right. They were fierce and strong together, and she only wished that what they had could last for ever.

'Will you be all right working on the island on your own when I have to leave?'

'What?' His question came as a complete surprise. 'Are you going somewhere?'

Luca's hesitation gave her the answer to that.

'You're still in charge of everything where the jewels are concerned while I'm away,' he reassured her as he planted a kiss on her lips.

'And I'm happy with that,' she confirmed.

'You don't sound happy.' Luca's dark eyes searched hers.

'But I am,' she said, trying to convince herself that this was true.

Email wasn't enough. Telephone calls were frustrating. What was even more frustrating was the way Jen could do exactly as she'd told him and immerse herself in her work to the exclusion of everything else, including him. He'd been away around a month now, and she still showed no sign of easing up on her schedule, or, more significantly, missing him.

'I'll be on the island next week…' He cursed viciously beneath his breath, realising how tense he had become as he waited for her to answer.

'That's great,' she said.

'But?' he queried, sensing there was something more coming.

He frowned as he thought what that could be. Stretching out his legs, he rested them on the desk and crossed his booted feet. It had been a long, hard day, with non-stop negotiations, but the deal was done. It was the biggest yet for his company, and he was ready to cut himself some down time, and yet he'd hardly touched the glass of whisky at his side, because he was waiting for Jen to say: 'Come now,' he realised. It would be even better had she added, 'Please don't wait until next week—I need to see you now—I need to talk to you—I need to feel your arms around me.' That was the way women usually behaved around him, and he had always found some excuse to keep his distance, but not this time, because this time he was hooked. And all Jen was giving him was silence. 'Something wrong, Jen?' he probed.

'We have a problem,' she said tensely.

He lowered his feet and sat up. 'Go on…'

'I can't catalogue some of these gemstones.'

'What do you mean? Can't you find any reference to them?'

'No. I mean they're stolen, Luca. I think you'd better get back here right away.'

Jen sat waiting tensely for Luca to arrive. It was early evening and still warm in the kitchen of the guest house. She was wearing the jeans and T-shirt she'd been wearing all day. It seemed more important to get the records she had compiled for him finished and printed out, rather than to put on any sort of show for Luca. He wouldn't appreciate it. Not today, because today he needed the business-orientated person she had fast become, not some fluffball swooning at his feet. She had a full set of records for him to study set out on the kitchen table in front of her with those entries that concerned her marked in red. There were a lot of entries marked in red.

Jen felt marked in red. She felt as if there were a big red cross on her forehead, marking her out as a gangster's moll, and the dupe of his father Don Tebaldi. What would her parents think of her now? What would Lyddie think? Her mother's career had been of the highest order, and blemish-free. They'd be heartbroken to think that what Jen had discovered could mean the end of her career. Any hint of dishonesty was the kiss of death in the world she hoped to enter, and she was sitting in front of a list of stolen property that, at her rough calculation, would be valued conservatively at several hundred million. How would Luca react to that? If he was implicated she'd know right away. She could read him.

How would she react to Luca when she saw him again after his absence? Her emotions were so pent up inside, she had no idea. She had dreamed about him every night. During the day when she was working, she'd weave fantasies around living a normal life, and maybe even building a happy family together. She always had been a dreamer, Jen concluded. Glancing at the damning list in front of her, she knew she couldn't even have told Lyddie about it. What she'd discovered was far too shocking. She was disappointed in herself for not seeing the risk sooner. No distinction would be made by the prosecution service if the stolen gems were discovered on Luca's property. Everyone involved would inevitably be tarred with the same brush. Jen's reputation would be ruined. No

smoke without fire, they'd say at the auction house. No
one would defend her. She could just imagine the direc-
tors running for cover.

'Jen?'

She sprang to her feet at the sound of Luca's voice. She
had been so lost in thought that she hadn't heard him arrive. Her determination to challenge him with what she'd
found counted for nothing when she saw him. She flew
to him and threw herself into his arms. 'I've missed you!'

'And I missed you,' Luca said fiercely, holding her
close. 'You have no idea how much.'

'You're squeezing the life out of me—'

'Then, I'll kiss you instead.'

He smothered her with kisses. Tears threatened, she
was so pleased to see him. Losing herself in his familiar
strength and heat was pure joy. He smelled so good, and
looked amazing, but then Luca always did, even when
he'd come straight from the office. There was no sign of
a power suit jacket, and his shirtsleeves were rolled up,
but he was still wearing the suit trousers. Had he been as
keen to see her, as Jen had been keen to see Luca? The
thought thrilled her. But now she had a duty to show him
what a mess his father had left behind. As she pulled
away from his embrace she felt terrible for him. Luca had
taken on so much since his father had left for Florida.
Maria had told her this, emphasising that he still had his
own business to run. It couldn't be helped, Jen thought,
picking up the records she'd compiled. Luca had to know
sooner or later that his father's hidden cache of jewels
contained more than one secret.

'Luca, I'm so sorry, but I'm afraid your father has left
more than you might have bargained for.'

He huffed a wry smile. 'Nothing you can tell me about
my father will come as a surprise to me. Don't worry.

I'll handle it. How have you been this past month? You look tired.'

Jen exhaled with weary amusement. 'I was going like a train, until I discovered this...' Concern covered her face as she handed Luca the papers.

'I appreciate your hard work,' he said, 'but I've travelled a long way—and to see you, not these.' He put the papers down and turned to her. 'Seems to me, my task is to make you forget them for one night.'

She was on the point of protesting that he must look at them now, but Luca's rapidly darkening stare stopped her.

'Don't you think I can distract you?' he said.

The hint of a smile on that firm, sexy mouth gave her no alternative.

'I wouldn't be surprised if you could,' she said.

They made love as if it were the first time, only now it was so much better, because now they knew each other's bodies, and she was at ease with Luca, and confident with him.

'I love you,' she murmured as they lay facing each other side by side. She laughed when Luca raised an amused brow. 'I'm sorry if that's too much information.'

'I love you too. And I'm not sorry if it's too much information,' Luca countered as he turned her beneath him.

Jen's world expanded like the unfurling petals of a flower. With those words, anything seemed possible. She wanted to say more to Luca, but he made words impossible. He was deep inside her, where she wanted him to be, and when they were one like this nothing else mattered.

Except that he loved her, Jen thought, basking in the knowledge, and that was all she had ever wanted—trust, closeness, oneness, and the rightness of being with the man she loved. It was enough for her. Nothing else could even come close. Words could never express how she felt about Luca, and she didn't need to tell him anything more, when her eyes must be telling him everything he needed to know.

They fell asleep in each other's arms with their limbs entwined in contented exhaustion. When she woke to the new day it was to find sunshine streaming through the open window. It was such a happy sight, she felt renewed in spirit in spite of her concerns about the jewels. It was as if anything was possible now Luca was back.

She couldn't remember ever being so optimistic, Jen thought as she crept out of bed. She didn't want to wake him as she went to grab a bottle of water from the console table by the wall. He looked so peaceful, lying with his arm above his head, and most of his magnificent body on show beneath the rumpled sheet. She stared at him for several moments. How could she resist him?

She couldn't, Jen concluded as she tiptoed back to bed.

Luca had laid an ambush, and now he shot up from the bed to drag her, screaming with happy excitement, into his arms.

'Did I frighten you?' he growled, teasing her unmercifully with the rasp of his stubble, and the touch of his hands.

'You know you did,' she accused, shrieking with thrilled outrage.

He swung her onto the bed at his side. 'So what are you going to do about it?' he challenged.

'It's what you're going to do about it that I'm interested in,' she said. 'I can only think that you will have to make up for shocking me with a prolonged exercise in pleasure.'

'No,' Luca protested as he covered his eyes with his forearm. 'Please don't send me to the salt mines again.'

'Then, make love to me instead,' she commanded.

'If I must.'

'You'd better,' she warned, laughing as Luca moved on top of her.

Was there anything better than this? Luca wondered as he rested his chin on the heel of his hand to watch Jen sleep. She was curled up in his arms where she'd drifted off. She hadn't stayed awake long enough to tell him he could stop. He smiled, doubting she would ever tell him to stop. He was inexhaustible and she was insatiable. It was an explosive combination, and one he had never found before. This was special. Jen was special. But relationships had to be founded on trust, and they had so many secrets. Jen telling him about his father's stolen gems had shocked him, whatever he'd said to her at the time, but at least she'd been absolutely straight with him, while his father had left him a criminal mess to sort out. Everything about her said that Jen would never try to trick his brother. The only thing he could do was to ask her straight what she knew about Raoul's will. His feelings for Jen were too strong to leave it any longer. He had to be as honest with her as she had been with him. She had saved him more trouble than she knew by spotting the discrepancies in the gemstones, and then telling him so promptly. He definitely owed her for that.

Luca was amazing. Not only was he amazingly gorgeous, and the best lover imaginable, as well as clever and funny, and warm, he was amazingly effective when it came to sorting out problems with the authorities. By midmorning the identities of the missing stones had been confirmed, and recovery had been arranged through Luca's security company so they could be returned to their rightful owners.

'You can stop worrying now,' he said as he cut the line to the last of the insurance companies. 'And you can still have your exhibition.' He came around the desk.

They had hunkered down in his study to get things sorted. Jen had been tensely perched on the edge of a chair throughout, but now she got up to exhale with relief.

'There are plenty of gemstones left for you to create the most fabulous display,' Luca reassured her, taking her into his arms. 'A couple of the insurance companies even suggested approaching the owners of the recovered stones to ask if you could exhibit them along with the rest. It would add to their notoriety and thus to their value, which in turn means higher insurance premiums for their owners.' He laughed as he said this. 'Win-win all round.'

'You nailed it,' she agreed.

'Thanks to you,' he said, dipping his head to kiss her once, and then again and again. 'You know, I never thought I'd say this,' he admitted when they finally broke apart.

'Say what?' Jen prompted.

'That I really love being with you.'

'That's it?' she demanded.

He teased her with a thoughtful look. 'That I love working with you?'

'I think you're being deliberately provocative.'

'That I love making love to you?'

'I should hope you do. And?' she prompted. Her eyes were probably shining like beacons in the night, which made a nonsense out of everything she'd ever read about hiding her feelings or holding back, but she couldn't help herself because she was in love with him, and she desperately wanted to hear Luca say again that he loved her too. His stare changed, heated. She knew those signs, and her body responded with enthusiasm. Seeing her answering fire, Luca swung her into his arms, and carried her out of the room. He ran up the stairs. They were both laughing, both on a high, celebrating life and each other.

'That I love reassuring you?' he suggested as he backed his way into the bedroom.

'Not enough,' Jen protested as he laid her down on the bed.

The look he gave her now said Luca knew exactly what was on her mind.

'Not nearly enough,' she complained, sitting up on the bed to brush her lips against his stubble-roughened cheek.

'Okay,' he agreed, pulling back and adopting a serious expression. 'I can see I'll have to do better.'

'You'll have to do a lot better,' she assured him as Luca began stripping off his clothes. 'I'm depending on it.'

She was naked seconds later. Stretching out his length against her, Luca drew her into his arms, and, cupping her face in his hands, he kissed her so tenderly that tears stung the backs of her eyes. She'd never been so happy. She'd never thought herself capable of experiencing anything like this.

Pulling back, Luca stared steadily into her eyes, and his expression had changed, from teasing to serious. 'I love you,' he said, and then his mouth tugged up at one corner as if he couldn't believe it, either. 'Just that,' he admitted. 'Pure and true. Love's more important than anything else, don't you agree?'

'Absolutely,' Jen whispered. 'Oh, yes, I certainly do.'

As he stroked Jen's hair after making his declaration, he wanted the moment to last for ever. He had never felt this close to anyone. He had never told a woman that he loved her, apart from his mother, and then he'd been a little boy, and that memory was a distant bell he could hardly hear now. Finding love with Jen was so unexpected it made it even more special. He wanted to frame the moment, and brand it on his mind. 'I love you,' he whispered again.

'We're stronger together than we are apart, for sure,' she said confidently.

He laughed. 'You're always so certain.'

'Yes. I am,' she agreed. 'Shouldn't I be?'

He kissed her to reassure her. 'Of course you should. Why not?'

'I don't know,' she said, frowning. 'You tell me...' She smiled trustingly into his eyes.

He might never get another moment like this. Their barriers were down and they were being completely honest with each other. He had been waiting for the right moment, and if he was ever going to ask Jen about Raoul's intentions, this was the right—the only moment?

'Is there anything you can tell me about Raoul's will that you might have forgotten?' he said.

Jen was sure her blood had been replaced by ice. She stared at Luca blankly. 'What do you mean?' Her voice barely made it to a whisper, and then that whisper was hoarse. She couldn't understand the question. What did he think she knew about his brother's will? The one thing she could be sure about was that Raoul would never put anything down in writing that might rebound on someone he cared deeply about.

'Jen?'

Luca was staring at her with that teasing, enquiring expression that she usually loved. It had always warmed and reassured her in the past, but right now it was doing the opposite. How could he think this was an appropriate time to ask the question? Her hands were shaking as she grabbed the sheet to cover herself.

'It's a simple question, Jen. All I'm asking is that you

tell me any detail that Raoul might have let slip about his will.'

'His will?' she repeated numbly.

'Yes—come on, Jen. Raoul talked to you—he must have mentioned it.'

'Must he?' She was still frowning, still confused, and no doubt staring at Luca like a complete idiot, which was how she felt, but not for the reasons he probably imagined. She could sense his impatience rising, which suggested Luca must have been brooding on this for some time. She didn't want to think too deeply about what that meant, or how it might affect the tender green shoot of their new relationship.

'Come on,' he prompted, smiling encouragement. 'I don't think I'm being unreasonable. You've already admitted that Raoul confided in you. He must have mentioned this—'

'I *admitted*?' she repeated, staring at Luca with fresh eyes. 'Am I being accused of something?'

'Don't be ridiculous,' he exclaimed, throwing himself off the bed. He began to pace. 'And don't look at me like that.'

'Like what?' she queried.

'As if you're seeing me for the first time.'

'Maybe I am.'

'Jen—'

'What?' Climbing off the bed, she took the sheet with her, winding it around her like a shroud. It was hard to walk, almost impossible, but the mere fact of arranging yards of white cotton so she could put some distance between herself and Luca gave her something else to concentrate on apart from the seething hurt inside her.

'Jen—please.' Coming to her side, Luca caught hold of her.

'Let me go,' she warned.

There was something in the tone of her voice that made him lift his hands away. Holding them up, palm flat in a sign of surrender, he demanded, 'What?'

She didn't trust herself to say anything. Whatever she said now could only sound bitter and hurt. She'd waited a month for Luca to come back, and now he had returned, the mistrust between them had erupted all over again.

CHAPTER FOURTEEN

SHE WAS SICK in the sink. She had retreated to the bathroom and locked the door. Luca was on the other side of the door, his voice ringing with concern. 'Jen? Are you all right in there?'

All right?

She was devastated. Luca's words kept washing over her in big, drowning waves. Raoul's will? What was behind the question? Did Luca think she had something to gain from Raoul's will? Raoul was broke, as far as she knew. That was what he'd told her. Raoul wouldn't lie to her. Why would he? She'd never believed in his so-called 'expectations'. Lots of gamblers kidded themselves about things like that. It hadn't mattered to Jen. She hadn't cared if he had money or not, apart from the fact that the lack of it had made things hard for Raoul. She'd tried to help him. She'd never judged people on what they were worth. She had never seen how that was relevant. She either liked people, or she didn't, and she had liked Raoul very much—

'Jen!'

Luca's shout seemed to be enough to upset her stomach again, and she lurched back to the sink just in time.

'Jen, answer me, or I'm coming in. I'll break the door down—'

'Leave me alone.'

'Jen—I'm warning you—'

'Shut up!' Her scream bounced off the walls, and it was she who kicked the door.

Sluicing her face in cold water, she dried her face and stared at her ashen reflection in the mirror with alarm. Grabbing a robe from the back of the door, she belted it securely. 'I'm coming out.'

Luca had tugged on his pants and stood towering over her like a monument to masculine pride. 'How dare you?' she challenged him. 'All this time when I thought we were getting closer, you've been brooding about your brother's will.'

'Forgive me, Jen—' Luca was as tense as she'd ever seen him. 'I haven't handled this well.'

'Understatement. I can't even get my head around it,' she admitted. 'You tell me you love me, and ten seconds later prove that your only concern is Raoul's money.' She made an involuntary sound of distress as she glanced at the rumpled bed. 'Was this all part of your master plan?'

'There is no master plan. There's a lot more to it than that.'

She huffed a humourless laugh. 'I'm sure there is.

'Raoul was a very wealthy man—'

Jen laughed with incredulity. 'You're just making it worse,' she exclaimed as she realised that feelings could change in a moment, and trust could be destroyed even faster than that.

Luca's stare didn't waver from her face. 'I can't avoid the truth.'

'And is that supposed to reassure me?' Jen exclaimed. 'And, by the way, are you talking on your own behalf, or for your father?'

'I represent the Tebaldi family. I'm protecting the family, as I always have.'

'From me?' Jen's lips felt numb. Luca's words had smashed every atom of feeling out of her. She had believed him when he said he loved her, and now this. 'I don't understand what you're getting at,' she admitted. 'If you could try to explain—'

'So you really know nothing?'

'Less than,' she stated, angry now. 'I didn't even know Raoul had a will. The subject never came up. Raoul was young. He didn't expect to die. And he didn't have any money, as far as I knew. You insist Raoul was a wealthy man? Then, why did he have to borrow money from me? He was grateful for a twenty, Luca. Does that sound like a man I called my friend for any reason other than he was a great guy?'

'I don't know,' Luca admitted.

'Well, that's a sad reflection on your relationship with your brother—and even worse on your true feelings when it comes to you and me.'

Hurt lashed through her when Luca remained silent. Raoul had seemed like a lost soul to Jen. He'd been uprooted, Raoul had told her, and longed for nothing more than acceptance from his family, so he could begin the long road to recovery from his gambling addiction with the help of true friends.'

'Raoul had substantial expectations,' Luca said at last.

'Expectations?' Jen repeated with a frown on her face. 'Yes. I remember Raoul's expectations, but I thought he was kidding himself.'

'No. My brother was about to become a very wealthy man.'

Jen shook her head with exasperation. 'You're making it all about money again.'

'Yes. I am.'

As this sank in she resented the fact that Luca had made her feel defensive and angry. 'How cold you make it sound—as if money could have saved your brother. I'll tell you what could have saved Raoul—love could have saved him. Understanding could have saved him. A few minutes of your precious time might have saved him—

'Don't! Take your hands off me!' she raged when Luca took hold of her shoulders to try and make her face him. 'Don't you ever touch me again. You have no right—'

As she flung herself out of his grip she saw Luca's grimace of pain, but it was too late for that, just as it was too late for either of them to revisit the past. They couldn't help Raoul any more than she could bring Lyddie back, and she would not have her friendship with Raoul tarnished by this talk of his money.

'What can I say to make things right?' Luca asked quietly, standing stiffly like a statue, alone and isolated.

'Nothing,' she said coldly. He might be used to solving every problem, but he couldn't solve this. What had happened to Luca's brother had to be agony for him, but Luca's remorse couldn't save him from the pattern she'd seen emerging. He'd been close to his brother, and had found it all too easy to pull away, and now he was doing the same to her. She had no intention of sticking around to be hurt and blamed to ease his guilt.

'Jen?'

Slamming a hand across her mouth, she rushed back to the bathroom. It had to be all the raised emotions getting to her, Jen reasoned, hoping she'd make it in time.

It was several minutes before Jen raised her head from the sink, and when she saw her green face in the mirror, she groaned. 'No. Please. No...' The emotional turmoil had been enough to churn her stomach, but this sickness had no connection with that, she suspected. It made perfect sense. Her hormones were all over the place. Her emotional outburst was just another symptom. She was pregnant with Luca's baby.

'Jen?' He was calling to her with more urgency now. 'Are you all right?'

'Go away!'

'I'm not going anywhere,' Luca assured her. 'I'm worried about you—'

'It's too late for that,' she assured him.

Never had a truer word been spoken, Jen thought tensely.

'We need to talk,' Luca insisted.

'I've got nothing to say to you.' She held her breath, hoping he would leave, while a really big part of her hoped that he wouldn't.

'Jen, I'm sorry—'

'Your apology might be more convincing, if you explained what you're trying to get at when you keep talking about your brother's money.'

'Come out of there, and we will talk. We can't discuss anything like this.'

She didn't dare to leave the sanctuary of the bathroom, not yet. She needed time for her stomach to settle, and time to compose herself so she could ask some sensible questions.

'Did you know Raoul made you the main beneficiary of his will?'

She slid down the wall to the floor. No. And she couldn't believe it. She didn't want to believe it. She didn't care about Raoul's money. It was the last thing on her mind.

'Did you hear me, Jen?'

She'd heard him, but she couldn't speak. She was over-

whelmed by grief for a man neither of them had been able
to save, and for a sister who would never see Jen's baby.

'I need a moment,' she choked out.

None of this made sense, Jen reflected. Raoul had left
everything to her? Raoul had left *what* to her? Raoul
didn't have any money. The only thing she could be sure
about was that she was as naïve in love as she was in life,
and now a baby would suffer because of it. Sucking in a
deep, steadying breath, she concentrated on settling her
stomach, wondering if it would behave long enough for
her to leave the bathroom so she could straighten things
out with Luca.

Some minutes passed, and then a few more, until finally she was as confident as she could be that the worst
of the sickness was over. Smoothing her hair, she chewed
some colour into her lips.

Cleaning her teeth, she swilled her mouth.

'Sorry,' she called out. 'I must have eaten something
that disagreed with me. I'll be right there.' Bracing herself, she opened the door. 'You were saying something
about Raoul's will?'

'I think we'd both better sit down.'

She confronted Luca's dark stare steadily. 'I'd rather
stand.'

Luca frowned, as if her cool tone surprised him. She
guessed he was surprised she could be so detached. He
should have realised that, like him, she had learned to
distance herself from feelings after the trauma of Lyddie's
death. She'd had to, or she'd have gone mad.

'Just tell me what you know about Raoul's will.'

'Very little,' she admitted. 'I shared a lot with your
brother, but not that. We never talked money—just that
one time when he needed my help.' She smiled faintly,

remembering Jay-Dee telling her that Raoul didn't even own the clothes he stood up in. He couldn't afford dry cleaning, and had regularly helped himself from Jay-Dee's wardrobe.

'Raoul's trust fund,' Luca prompted tensely. 'He must have told you something about it?'

'Nothing.' Jen's mind raced to confirm that this was true. 'Raoul never mentioned a trust fund. I didn't know anything about it.'

'And no reason why you should,' Luca agreed.

'So what's this about, Luca?' She badly needed to sit down. Standing after being so sick was making her feel faint again. She discreetly steadied herself on the arm of a chair.

She should have known he'd spot the momentary weakness, and Luca was at her side within a moment. There was a long silence, and then he said, 'Do you think you're pregnant?'

'What?' Jen had her own suspicions, but she wasn't ready to share them with Luca. 'First the trust fund and now this? Have you got any more accusations up your sleeve?'

'I'm not *accusing* you of being pregnant. I'm just asking the question. I recognise the signs—'

'That's a bold claim for a man to make,' she interrupted. All her hurt spilled out at once. 'How many women have you got pregnant?'

'None,' Luca said, looking genuinely shocked at her barb. 'And you haven't answered my question,' he reminded her quietly. 'Do you think you could be pregnant?'

'Do you care?'

'Of course I care! *Dio*, Jen! I can't believe you're asking me that. Do I look like a man who wouldn't care for the mother of his child?'

'I don't know,' Jen said honestly, still reeling from the shock of her own suspicion that she might be pregnant. 'I don't know if you're capable of feeling. Your family history certainly doesn't point to it.'

'My father might have found it impossible to love anything more than himself, or his hoard of jewels, but that doesn't mean I'll repeat his mistakes. I've learned from the past. I haven't been damaged by it.'

'Are you saying I have?' Jen's hands balled into tight, angry fists. Luca was forcing her to confront a truth she had always shied away from.

'I'm saying you were forced to take on a lot at an early age,' he said gently. 'I'm saying there was never anyone for you to turn to.'

'I didn't need anyone's help,' she protested.

'I think you still blame yourself for your sister's death.'

'What?' She could feel the blood draining out of her face.

'You can't deny it,' he insisted. 'When the judge ruled in your favour, it was supposed to be for ever—that's what you believed. You and Lyddie would live happily ever after—'

'Stop it!' she begged, but he wouldn't stop.

'When we were sharing things, you told me how hard you fought to keep the two of you together when your parents died. You must have felt that your world had come to an end when your sister was killed too.'

She was sobbing openly now.

'You were left with a gaping hole you thought you'd never fill—'

'You don't know anything about my feelings,' Jen exclaimed, wheeling away to hide the emotion swamping her.

'It was an accident, Jen,' Luca insisted. Taking hold

of her shoulders, he turned her to face him. 'Your sister's death was a tragic accident. You can't hold yourself responsible for that.'

He stopped as Jen made a defensive gesture as if she couldn't bear to hear any more.

'Is avoiding the truth the legacy your sister would have wanted to leave?' he asked after a few tense seconds had passed. 'You knew her better than anyone.'

'Yes, I did,' Jen returned fiercely. 'So I'd appreciate it if you'd keep your theories to yourself.'

'Would she want you to ignore what your heart's telling you?'

'And what is that, exactly?' she demanded tensely.

'That you love me, and I love you, which means we have to be honest with each other.'

'I am being honest with you,' she exclaimed in a tone hoarse with emotion.

'Are you? Why didn't you tell me you were a virgin the first time we made love?'

'What?'

'Didn't you think I'd know?' Luca shook his head. 'I'm not proud of what I did, because I suspected all along, and then I knew for sure, but it still didn't stop me.'

'I didn't want you to stop.'

'I won't use that as an excuse. I'm trying to show you that, whatever you think of me, I only have your best interests at heart. There are things I can't tell you,' he admitted, 'not until I understand Raoul's intentions. I get that you're still suffering the loss of your sister. These things only ease with the passage of time, and two years isn't that long. I get that you don't know who to trust, or what to believe, but please—'

Her bitter laugh cut him off. 'Are you asking me to trust you?'

'Yes. If you're having my baby, of course I am.' Catching hold of her, he brought her in front of him. 'Nothing is as important to me as that, but I do have to get my brother's will sorted out, and anything you can tell me might just help. Can't you see how important you are to me? You're everything, Jen.'

He meant every word. If Jen was expecting his child—*his child*—she was the centre of his universe.

The future flashed in front of Jen's eyes. For all the fierce pride reflected on Luca's face at the possibility that he might be about to become a father, he was still suspicious, or why was he continuing to ask her so many questions? If she reacted angrily now, and pushed him away, there would be constant battles ahead of them. If she were pregnant, those battles would impact on their child.

He made things easier when he drew her close, and, in a voice of infinite tenderness, breathed against her hair, 'I'm sorry, Jen. You must think I'm always challenging you, but there's so much I don't understand about my brother's life, and you're the only one who can fill in those gaps.'

'I'm sorry too,' Jen said honestly. 'I'm sorry it's come to this, with us fighting each other. I'm sure it's the last thing Raoul would have wanted.'

'If you're pregnant you can blame your hormones,' Luca said, holding her so he could stare wryly into her face, 'but I have no excuse.'

'Apart from your love for your brother,' she said. 'It's hard to forgive you for not trusting me,' Jen said honestly. 'And I can't pretend I'm not shocked by Raoul's last wishes, but you have to believe me when I say I had absolutely no idea he was going to do this—'

As emotion overwhelmed her, she swayed, and Luca caught her.

'Forget it,' he said. 'You've had enough stress for one day.' Bringing her close, he kissed the top of her head. 'I promise you this...if I have to spend the rest of my life making up for what you've been through, I will. You're far too important to me to let anything get in the way.'

Luca's eyes had changed, darkened, and she had no strength left to fight him. She did feel faint. And she did feel hurt. She was still angry with him for not trusting her, but they'd both suffered so much grief, and neither of them had ever had the chance to express it before. If ever there was time for understanding, it was now. The only time she felt comforted was when she was in Luca's arms. And he was so gentle with her now as he dipped his head to kiss her that she had to respond. He kept on kissing her and reassuring her with words that eventually made her smile, and then those words changed to whispered suggestions that made her body yearn for him. Feeling her soften, his hands moved from cupping her face to cupping her naked breasts beneath the towelling robe. He knew exactly what to do, and exactly what to say to add to her mounting arousal. And when her legs weakened and she exhaled on a shaking breath, he lifted her into his arms and carried her to bed.

CHAPTER FIFTEEN

GENTLE LOVEMAKING COULD be as pleasurable as any other type of lovemaking, maybe even more so, Jen discovered. She and Luca had been fierce together, sleepy in bed, and had made love up against a wall. He had taken her over a sofa, in the shower and on the floor, but this steady rhythm, so smooth and slow, and yet so firm and dependable, was the most extreme build up to release she'd known yet. It was certainly the most emotional. Staring into each other's eyes as the pleasure built required every bit of control she possessed. She wanted to move fiercely, and greedily claim her reward, but the look in Luca's eyes told her to hold on just a little longer, and then a little longer still. She groaned and begged him shamelessly for release.

'Not yet,' he whispered, pinning her arms above her head so he could kiss her lips, her eyes, her brow, her neck, her breasts.

'When?' She opened her legs a little wider, as wide as she could for him, pressing her thighs apart to isolate the area of pleasure he was attending to so expertly. She felt so deliciously sensitive there, which made the torture of being forced to wait for release almost painfully extreme.

She was as high as it got on a plateau of pleasure,

waiting—longing to fall off—when Luca whispered, 'Now...'

She didn't have to think about it. That one word was enough to send her rocketing into the wildest release yet. She bucked repeatedly, crying out with shocked delight as he held her in place to make sure she received every last, delicious pulse of pleasure. Before the waves of that release had a chance to subside, he was moving again, firmly and reliably to the same deliciously dependable rhythm.

It was a long time after that, when they were lying together with their limbs entwined, and Luca's arms were cradling her close to his chest, that she told him on an exhausted smile, 'You're amazing.'

'And you're beautiful.'

She laughed at that, knowing it wasn't true, but Luca's gaze remained steady on her face. Brushing her mouth with his lips until she was groggy with love for him, he murmured, 'And soon to be so fabulously wealthy as well.'

Jen stiffened, her love-fogged brain clicking into gear. 'Wealthy?' she said. 'Please—not that again.'

'Raoul's will...we have to talk about it some time.'

'But not now,' she said. Hurt obliterated the calm state of happiness she'd been basking in after making love. It was as if she had never relaxed, and Luca had never made love to her, and she was right back to feeling as she had when he'd first mentioned the wretched will. 'I think you'd better explain,' she said angrily, putting as much distance between them as she could.

'You really don't know?'

'I really don't know,' she confirmed tensely, dreading what might come next. Shuffling up in the bed, she wrapped the bedclothes around her.

'I accept you don't know about Raoul's will—'

'That's very good of you.' Smoothing her hair, she turned away as Luca rolled over and sat up at her side.

'I was so sure Raoul must have confided in you.'

'Confided what?' she exclaimed. 'We never discussed his will. Why would we? And what are we doing in bed together, if all you want to talk about is that?' She stared at him accusingly. 'I thought we'd settled this. I can't believe I've fallen for it again.'

'Fallen for what?' he said as she leapt off the bed.

'For you—and your lies,' she shouted back at him as she stumbled her way to the bathroom with the sheet tangled around her feet.

'Raoul was on the point of becoming very wealthy when he died—'

Luca's voice stopped her at the bathroom door.

'He'd gone through one fortune, but only had six months to wait until his thirtieth birthday when he would have gained access to his trust.'

'Six months,' Jen repeated tensely.

'That's right. And then his problems would have been over.'

'So in the same length of time you estimated my work here would take, Raoul's trust would be released. To me,' she added coldly. 'That's why you wanted me here, wasn't it, Luca?' she said, turning to face him. 'Everything else was just a ruse. You had a few months to play with, and while I was here you expected to get a confession out of me—something to the effect that I had somehow persuaded your brother to make me the main beneficiary of his estate. Then you thought I'd accept a pay-off and disappear. Is that it, Luca?' She shook her head. 'You don't even need to say a word. I can see the truth in your eyes.'

She drew a deep, shaking breath. 'How could you?' she demanded in a voice made harsh with anger and grief.

'We didn't know you then. Try to understand my concerns for my father—'

'Your father?' she exclaimed with outrage.

'He was concerned about Raoul's expectations—'

'Raoul's expectations?' she interrupted as Luca continued to pull on his clothes. 'Your brother's problems went a lot deeper than money. And from what I've seen of his family, I think mine do too.' She felt duped and betrayed, and was only holding onto her control by her fingertips. 'Why didn't you bring this up before I came to Sicily? You could have asked me straight out at the club.'

'I didn't know you as well as I do now.'

'You didn't trust me,' she fired back.

'I wasn't sure of you,' Luca conceded.

'And now?' The cold had returned to her veins, but now it was ice. 'You made love to me, Luca. I could be having your baby. But all the time I was falling in love with you, you were keeping me here to suit your own ends. With less than six months to go before I inherited Raoul's trust fund, you must have been under real pressure.' Jen blenched as she thought about it. 'But you were determined to use every one of those months, if you had to, weren't you, to find out what I knew?'

With a disgusted shake of her head, she snatched up her clothes as emotion threatened to overwhelm her. 'You've been manipulating me all along. You said you loved me. You talked as if you knew how hard it was for me to express my feelings after Lyddie's death. We'd both shared such a terrible loss, I thought we understood each other, but now I can see that you were just trying to win my trust so I'd open up to you. You must have been surprised when your skills as a security expert failed to unmask the villain in your brother's life—'

'Jen, wait—' Luca's arm snapped out to keep her with him.

'I've done nothing wrong,' she exclaimed angrily, shaking him off. 'Let me go!'

The moment Luca released her, Jen finished dressing with shaking hands. 'I want you to leave now,' she said, pointing at the door.

'I'm not going anywhere,' Luca assured her. In a couple of strides, he was at her side. 'Your pregnancy—if there is a child—changes everything.'

'Yes, it does,' Jen agreed. 'It allows me to see what a fool I've been. Just the possibility that I might be pregnant has woken me up faster than I would have believed possible, and the first thing it tells me is that I don't want you involved—'

'If you're pregnant, I am involved,' Luca assured her. 'Even you can't change that.'

'I can keep you at a distance,' Jen countered. 'I'll be qualified soon, and I've got a guaranteed job at the auction house where they'll have to pay me more. I won't need you, your money, or anything else to do with the Tebaldi family.'

Luca ground his jaw, refusing to answer. 'Who will look after your baby while you work?'

'The company crèche,' she said, blessing Smithers & Worseley for being on the ball where that was concerned. 'I can continue to work after my mat' leave with the reassurance of knowing my child is in the same building. So, you see, Luca, I really don't need you at all.'

'You don't have a choice,' he said coldly.

'Really?' Jen challenged tight-lipped. 'Would you care

to put that to the test? Let me tell you one thing, Luca—you and your father don't frighten me.'

'What do you mean by that?'

'You said you would never take over from your father, but I don't think I believe you now.'

'Then, you're wrong,' he said quietly. 'I am Don Tebaldi's son, but that is a very different thing from being in business with my father, or taking over from him. My world and his are as different as could be, and if you're suggesting that I would sink to his tactics you couldn't be more wrong.'

'So keeping me here in the hope I might confess to something is different? It's not kidnap, or restraint. No,' she declared hotly. 'It's something far cleverer than that. It's subtle coercion, and not so subtle manipulation, and neither of those things is good in my book. Do you really think that after this I'd allow you to have any part in my life, or that of my child?' She laughed bitterly. 'You've tried to catch me out. I can see that now. But how am I supposed to confess to something when I don't know what that something is?' She shook him off when Luca attempted to soothe her. 'What was your aim, Luca? Were your father's instructions to stop at nothing until I signed a waiver relinquishing all claim on Raoul's estate?'

'I've told you before. I protect my father, but he doesn't instruct me—'

'Clearly not,' she flashed. 'Because you had a better solution: bring me to the island on any pretext, and then seduce me—win my trust and make me believe I can confide anything in you, because you *love* me.' She spat out the word. 'The Emperor's Diamond and all that nonsense was just to keep me busy until you could solve the puzzle of your brother's will.'

'Try to see things from my point of view—'

'Why should I?' she demanded.

'Because you cared for Raoul, and there had to be a very good reason why Raoul wrote his will in that particular way, and I'm trying to fathom out what that is. Don't you want to know? Think about it, Jen—think back. What was Raoul trying to achieve when he drew up his will in your favour?'

'Maybe I had time for him? Maybe Raoul thought I would use the money to help people like him—people with addictions. I don't know,' Jen admitted. Angry as she was, what Luca had said did bear thinking about. But then something else occurred to her. 'I hope you're not suggesting I was blackmailing your brother?'

'No,' he exclaimed with what she thought was genuine shock. 'Of course not.

'I can see that my father's intolerance, coupled to my brother's desperate need for his love and acceptance, could lead you to think Raoul might be the perfect target for blackmail by someone,' he admitted, 'but I would never believe that of you. Anyone could have told my father anything, and it wouldn't have made one jot of difference to his contempt for us. He despised both his sons, especially Raoul. And, no, I don't think you've been underhand in any way. You couldn't possibly have predicted that Raoul would be killed in a street race. No one could.'

A tense silence fell between them, but then, as they were both letting all the poison out, Jen voiced a fear she had so far kept to herself. 'Raoul lived life on the edge. We both know it. Do you think he might have driven recklessly that night because he wanted to kill himself?'

'What?' Luca exclaimed softly.

'I think Raoul was so desperate for love, and for support and understanding, he was at his wits' end.' Jen fell silent. She'd said enough. Luca's face was a mask of shock. This time the silence went on and on, and in the end she had to say something. 'I can't say anything more,' she explained, 'without breaking my promise to Raoul.'

'Your promise?' Luca flared. 'Always another secret with you, Jen!' With an angry gesture, he exclaimed, 'Your promise to a dead man doesn't count.'

'Don't—' Shocked by Luca's outburst, she turned away.

Jen's reaction shamed him. He hadn't exactly covered himself with glory. 'I'm trying to understand,' he explained, making one last desperate attempt to find out more. 'I'm trying to understand my brother. I'm hungry for information. If I've shocked you I'm sorry. I just want to make sure my brother's last wishes are honoured, and to do that I have to know what you know. Please. This is the last thing I can ever do for him.'

Jen didn't speak on her way to the door. She stood beside it, trembling with emotion as she waited for Luca to leave. 'I'll finish cataloguing the jewels,' she said. 'And I'll arrange your exhibition. But then I'm going home. I'll let you know if I'm pregnant as soon as I've seen a doctor. If I am expecting your child, we'll have a meeting in England to decide where we go from there—where *I* go from there,' she amended before he had chance to speak.

'What about the money?' he said. 'Raoul's money?'

Jen stared at him with barely concealed contempt. 'Raoul's money?' she repeated.

'The six months will be up soon,' he reminded her, 'and then the trust will be released.'

'Are you going to make me an offer?' she challenged coldly.

That was exactly what his father had wanted him to do. 'No, of course not.'

'Then, why are you still here?'

'Jen, I—'

'Please leave.'

'I can't,' he said. 'Not before I know why Raoul wanted you to have the money. Please. Let me speak,' he insisted, when Jen tried to interrupt him. 'I think Raoul wanted you to have that money for a specific reason, and I don't know what that reason is, except he didn't entrust his thoughts to me or to my father, which means it was a cause dear to his heart that he only shared with you. If you're right when you say Raoul wanted to die, I can only imagine the depths of his desperation, and it's up to me *and* you to discover what he wanted you to do with his money.'

'If I knew something outside my promise to Raoul, I'd tell you,' she said, keeping her word to his brother to the end. 'And one more thing—I'll work faster and more efficiently on the exhibition if you and I keep our distance for a while.'

He almost smiled at the thought that he was getting dumped—would have smiled, if the situation hadn't been so tragic. He couldn't even argue with Jen. He'd had the same thought. There was so much emotional turmoil swirling around that if they didn't put some space between them, they would both implode. His body argued with the arrangement, but for her sake he overruled his body this time.

'I'll let your PA know when I'm ready to leave,' she said coolly.

'Shirley will arrange the jet for you,' he acknowledged in the same considered tone, hardly believing that he was offering to help Jen leave him.

'I'll book a regular flight when I'm ready, thank you,' she told him without emotion.

Jen was starting off as she meant to continue, with her

pride intact, and her integrity unchallenged. He could only admire her for that.

'I'll leave a forwarding number, so you can call to find out about the baby—or the lack of one,' she added quietly.

Her detachment didn't surprise him. Switching off was the only way he knew to handle the situation. They both had trust issues. Maybe they always would.

'I'll say goodbye, then,' he said.

If he had expected some reaction beyond a curt, 'Goodbye, Luca,' he was to be disappointed. Jen couldn't even bring herself to look at him.

CHAPTER SIXTEEN

Six months later...

THREE WORDS. THREE WORDS emailed to his business account.

Pregnancy progressing well.

Sitting back in his office chair, he swore softly. Jen's communications were regular, but terse. He supposed he couldn't blame her, though when each one arrived he couldn't help but feel shut out of the pregnancy she'd had confirmed within days of arriving back in London. He couldn't fault her for keeping him in the loop, but she didn't want anything more from him, she'd said. He'd been working. She'd been working.

Incredibly, with everything she'd taken on, Jen had completed her college course, graduating *summa cum laude*, thanks to work of the highest quality, Shirley had told him. But Jen had pushed him away. She hadn't wanted him at the ceremony, Shirley had told him. Echoes of how he'd treated Raoul couldn't be avoided. Shirley had Jen's number, in case of an emergency, but Jen never picked up when he called.

She'd left a legacy on the island in the form of a glit-

tering, world-class display of jewels in a new secure unit
that had been built especially to house them. He'd rather
they'd remained in the hessian sacks and Jen had stayed
with him. He couldn't see any difference between jewels
displayed in a vault, or jewels under the bed. They were
still hidden away. Like their feelings, he reflected grimly.

According to his sources Jen had released his brother's money, and had moved it to a private account where
it was being well managed. She hadn't touched a penny.
Why? He had no idea. The only certainty was that Jen
would never trust him again. He had pushed her once too
often on Raoul's secrets. He had arranged for the best
medical attention money could buy, but Jen had said she
preferred to use her local doctor. She attended the mid-
wife's clinic at the surgery on a regular basis, queuing for
her turn like everyone else, Shirley told him. He'd asked
Shirley to make sure Jen knew that everything she could
possibly need was only a phone call away. He was still
waiting for that call.

Jen sent on any medical reports she received, but addressed them to Shirley, who passed them on to him. He
could sense Jen's happiness in the impending birth, but
he felt cruelly, yet justifiably excluded. The most significant of those reports had included a note from Jen,
asking Shirley if she thought he'd want to know the sex
of his child.

What?

He wanted more than that. He wanted everything.

Shutting down his computer, he shoved his chair back
impatiently and stood. Digging his hands into his pockets, he went to lean his forehead against the cold glass
that was the only thing separating him from rolling black
thunderclouds on the other side of the window of his top-
floor office in Rome.

Decision made, he pulled out his phone.

Six hours to fuel the jet and file a flight plan? 'Two,' he barked. Weather conditions might be bad, but he needed to be in London now, not some time tomorrow.

The flight was everything he deserved. By the time he landed, the weather conditions had been dubbed the storm of the century. His was the last plane in before the airport closed its runways. He passed through security smoothly and his limousine was waiting at the kerb. He glanced at his wristwatch. Shirley had told him that Jen was determined to work right up to the birth, and that tonight she was working in the office at the casino, which meant she spent less time on her feet.

She shouldn't be working at all, he raged inwardly. And at the casino, where fights had been known to break out? She was seven months pregnant, for goodness' sake!

'As fast as you can,' he told the driver, remaining on the edge of his seat.

How would Jen respond to him after all this time? She might not even agree to see him. He ground his jaw with impatience as his driver threaded the big car skilfully through the tightly packed evening traffic. A lot could happen in six months. His father had died, leaving him properties across the world. He'd sold some of them, using the proceeds for his charities. He'd kept the island and the old house, and not for sentimental reasons, but because he could see a purpose for them. It was hardly a small step from that, to imagining Jen back on the island, taking a full part in his plans—if he could ever persuade her to come back with him.

Most of the arguments she could put up against that idea were gone. With his father's death everything had changed. There would never be razor wire, or security guards with guns patrolling the island again. Instead, there were flowers and lawns and tennis courts, two swimming pools, a baseball court, stables, and volley-ball on the beach. Jen's exhibition was open to the public so people could view them free of charge. The Emperor's Diamond with its infamous history took pride of place.

He wanted her to see what a success her exhibition had become, and had sent a handwritten note, inviting her to return to do just that, but she had declined his invitation, saying she was too busy with the Queen's Diamonds. The entire world knew about this very special exhibition for the Queen of England, and he could see that it was quite a step up for Jen, from sifting through his father's hessian sacks. She was now part of a team of experts from Smithers & Worseley tasked with displaying the Queen's Diamonds at the royal palace in London.

Undaunted by her refusal, he had sent a second note to let her know that the island had recently been deemed a heritage site, and that he'd named the summer camp for troubled youngsters after his brother. There was just one thing missing, and that was Jen. He didn't put that in his message. He had confined himself to the bare facts, as she did.

Another note from Luca. She couldn't wait to print it out. This was ridiculous, Jen thought as she waited for the club's printer to spew out Luca's text message so she could keep it with all the rest. She knew she was being ridiculous. What was the point of keeping them? What was she going to do with six months' worth of terse messages printed out on pristine sheets of A4?

'Do you want a ribbon for that?'

Jen glanced up as Jay-Dee walked into the office. 'Silly.'

'Not so,' Jen's good friend argued, leaning forward

to brush Jen's cheek with a fond kiss. 'All the best love letters should be tied up with pink ribbon.'

'Even when the message reads: Island now officially a Heritage Site. Raoul Tebaldi's Summer Camp in full swing—or it will be when I unblock the drainage.?'

'Eeeugh!' Jay-Dee exclaimed, recoiling in theatrical horror. 'You're right. Maybe leave that out?'

'You should read the rest,' Jen joked.

'You've kept them all?'

'What do you think?'

'Come here, baby…'

Sometimes, there was nothing better than being enveloped in a Jay-Dee hug.

His worst fears were confirmed when the limo drew up outside the club.

'No more punters tonight,' the tough guy on the door told him. 'There's been some trouble inside the club. The police have been called. Sorry, sir—'

'My girlfriend's in there—I'm here to get her out.'

A look and a firm handshake, during which the transfer of money took place, assured Luca's smooth passage into the club. It wasn't entirely trouble free, as he was the only one trying to get in, while a flood of people were fighting to get out. Once inside, he took in the scene at a glance.

A gang of drunken youths had surrounded one of the waiters and were baiting him with cruel gags. To Luca's horror, everyone had deserted the waiter, with the exception of the female manager, whom he remembered from his first visit to the casino, the maître d' and Jen—a heavily pregnant Jen—who, to his horror, was shielding the waiter with her body while screaming blue murder at the men. One of the bullies, blinded by drink, looked as if he was about to take a swing, regardless of the fact that there was a vulnerable woman in his way—

In a couple of strides he took the bully by the scruff of the neck. Putting himself and the thug between the gang and their victims, he was ready when the rest of the men attacked. Their mistake. He was heavily out-numbered, but a ferocious father hadn't trained Luca to fight when he was a boy only for Luca to let that train-ing go to waste now. Unarmed combat was his special-ity. At one time it had been his pleasure. He felt some of that satisfaction tonight.

Using the bully as a battering ram, he drove off the squealing men with the addition of a few well-aimed punches. It was all over when one of them came at him from behind. He turned to land a punch, but the waiter got there before him.

'Good shot,' he approved as the bully collapsed to the floor at his feet.

'Are you all right?' He swept a still-steaming Jen under the protection of his arm as he went to check the other victims of the gang. The maître d' and the female manager were both shaken up, and breathless with shock, but otherwise unharmed. The waiter—Jay-Dee, Jen ex-plained when she introduced them—was nursing a badly bruised knuckle.

'I didn't know I had it in me,' Jay-Dee commented with surprise, frowning as he checked his manicure.

'Well, thanks for your help,' Luca said as he shot a glance around the club to make sure they'd swept up all the gang. 'You saved the day.'

'Oh, I think you did that,' Jay-Dee argued, raising a brow as he glanced at Jen.

'Well, thank you for your assistance anyway—much

appreciated,' Luca stated as they exchanged a firm hand-shake.

'And hello to you too,' Jen murmured dryly as he ush-ered her away. 'That was quite an entrance.'

'In the nick of time, it seems to me,' he said grimly. 'Why are you still working?'

'Why are you still patronising me? I'm pregnant, not sick. You can't march back into my life and start telling me what to do.'

'You're in no state to take on a team of drunks,' he argued, drawing Jen into the office.

'And what would you do if your friend was threat-ened and insulted?' Jen challenged with passion as soon as the door was closed. 'Would you walk away? Would you turn your back?'

'I'm not seven months pregnant,' he pointed out, as his fears for Jen's safety vied with the way he felt being close to her again. 'I've missed you,' he said gruffly.

There was a silence during which he thought his world might come to an end, and then she whispered, 'I've missed you too.'

His relief was indescribable. It filled him, over-whelmed him, and made sense of life, giving him a rea-son to live, not on his own now, but with this woman and their child—if she'd have him, which was by no means certain.

'Thank you.'

His head lifted as she spoke.

He held her stare through the knock on the door.

'Aren't you going to answer it?' she said.

Frustration to be alone with Jen was eating him alive, but it was Jay-Dee, the heroic waiter, asking for a meet-ing before he left the club.

'Of course. Come in.'

'I've confirmed with Tess that we can use her office,' Jay-Dee explained to Luca, shooting a glance at Jen. 'Tess has assured us that we won't be disturbed.'

They sat around the pockmarked desk beneath the reluctant glimmer of a tacky chandelier. Jay-Dee sat behind the desk. Luca was fine with that, because it meant he could sit close to Jen on the other side.

'This might come as a shock to you,' Jay-Dee began. 'I don't know how much you knew about your brother, or what his last wishes might have been?'

'I've seen the will,' he said succinctly. His heart leapt in expectation of understanding the mystery surrounding Raoul's last testament.

'Raoul was sick,' Jay-Dee revealed with matching economy. 'He didn't have long to live,' he added bluntly.

Luca felt such a jolt that it took all he'd got not to show his shock, or his horror at the knowledge that his brother had been suffering, while he had been standing on his pride. There was no hint of recrimination in Jay-Dee's voice, and certainly no pity; he deserved none.

'He was ashamed of his illness,' Jay-Dee revealed in the same emotion-free tone.

'Ashamed?' He couldn't hide his shock this time.

'He'd contracted the illness before he met me. He told Jen and me about it, but Raoul didn't want anyone else to know. We kept the faith,' Jay-Dee finished quietly.

They both had, he thought, glancing at Jen, whose concerned gaze was fixed on Jay-Dee.

'Raoul didn't want to be a burden to any of us,' Jay-Dee continued, and with a slight break in his voice, he added, 'We loved each other.'

There was silence as the three of them turned over their thoughts, and then Jay-Dee said in the same candid tone, 'Even I didn't know everything about your brother's intentions, until after what would have been Raoul's thirtieth birthday, when I received a letter from his lawyer. Your coming here has saved me a trip to find you in Sicily,' he told Luca, attempting a laugh that ended up sounding more like a sob. 'Don't be angry with Jen,' he added in a shaking voice. 'She's been loyal to a fault.'

Jay-Dee and Jen exchanged a look so full of trust and love that Luca instantly envied it above all things.

'Raoul left me a letter, which his lawyer sent on,' Jay-Dee explained. 'He was worried that if he left his money to me the truth about our relationship would come out. He thought this would cause more pain for his family, and that it might put me in danger from his father. He understood his father's prejudices, and he didn't want you to be involved in yet another family conflict. I'm sorry to be so blunt about this Luca, but I owe you an explanation.'

'You don't owe me anything,' Luca said quietly.

He couldn't feel worse, knowing he'd deserted his brother. He could only be glad that Jay-Dee had been there for Raoul. He welcomed the man's candour, as he had always welcomed Jen's honesty. These were people he could work with, he thought.

'Your brother asked me to head up a summer camp for young people on the island,' Jay-Dee continued, 'but I don't have the business know-how to use his money in the way he would want. I knew none of this when you came to the club that night. I thought Raoul had left me. I didn't want to mention it, or him, or think of it again, because it hurt too much. Now I know he was only trying to protect me. Yes,' he added, seeing Luca's surprise. 'Raoul left everything to Jen so that when he died, I would be protected. He believed his father would come after me, all guns blazing, quite literally, if he knew about us.'

'You could have put Jen in danger too,' Luca said sharply.

'I knew nothing about Raoul's will, any more than Jen did,' Jay-Dee explained. 'I had no idea what he intended until I received that letter from his lawyer.'

'Luca, please—'

Jen pacified him with a look long enough for Jay-Dee to admit bluntly, 'I'd like to work with you, and so would Jen.'

His heart banged in his chest as he looked at her. 'Is this true?'

'If you'll have me.' A tender smile hovered hopefully around her mouth.

'I'm already planning to open a camp on the island that carries my brother's name,' he admitted, frowning.

'But do you have a scholarship programme?' Jen interrupted. 'Jay-Dee and I would like to use your brother's money for that. That's why I haven't touched it. I think it needs all three of us on the board, so we can work together in Raoul's name.'

He sat back and thought about this. It took him barely a few seconds to decide.

'That's a very good idea. Why don't we change the name to the Raoul Tebaldi and Lyddie Sanderson scheme?'

Jay-Dee had left them when Jen reached for Luca's hand. She guided it to the swell of her belly, where their son was kicking three bells out of her in an attempt, Jen decided in her crazy way, to reach his father—having recognised Luca as such, of course, being such an advanced child, even in the womb.

'What shall we call him?' she asked as Luca froze, with his hard face softened to an incredible degree.

Luca's answer was to kneel at her side. Turning to look at her, he cradled her face between his hands, and with the utmost reverence and tenderness he brushed his lips very lightly against hers. 'Let's call him Luciano, the bringer of light, Luci for short—unless you have a better idea?'

'I think Luci's perfect,' Jen agreed.

'Will you come home with me?' Luca asked, frowning as he stood. Reaching out his hands, he helped Jen to her feet.

'You have a home in London?' she asked.

He smiled. 'I do. But once your work on the exhibition for the Queen's Diamonds has been completed, I hope you'll come home to Sicily with me?'

Six months apart had been worse than a life sentence for Jen. To have parted on such bitter terms from Luca had left her bruised and hurt. To hear him issue this invitation now was like the cell door flying open, but before she stepped out she had to hear him say that there was more between them than mistrust over his brother's will. She wanted to hear him talk about love, and what the future held for them and their child, as well as the island.

'You're right to hesitate,' he said when she remained silent. 'I have no right to ask this of you. I have no right to ask anything of you. I've treated you abysmally. And I'll make no excuses,' he said, holding up his hand when she wanted to reassure him. 'I talked about money and I doubted you. I was sick with grief at losing the brother I had somehow lost in life, and lost again in death, but that wasn't your fault. I've thought of nothing but you for these past six months—you and our child. Living apart from you has been my punishment, and I only hope you can forgive me, so that my punishment can end.'

'So much misunderstanding,' Jen whispered. 'The

past has conditioned us both to look for trouble, and not to give our trust lightly, but we have to move on.'

'I don't deserve you—'

'To the future,' she said.

'So you'll come back with me?'

The expression on Luca's face told her everything she needed to know. 'I'd love that,' she said honestly, staring into his eyes. 'I love you.'

'You have no idea how much I love you,' Luca assured her fervently. 'And I'm looking forward to working with you so much.'

'Just to working with me?' Jen teased gently as Luca took her in his arms.

'I'm looking forward to making love to you most of all,' he admitted wickedly, and when she softened in his arms he kissed her again, and this time the kisses went on and on, until he pulled back, when Jen frowned and asked him, 'Won't the bump be a problem?'

'*Cara*, nothing on this earth is going to stand between me, and your pleasure. Shall we go...?'

Sometimes sleeping in a man's arms told you more about the man than hours of conversation, Jen decided. Sleeping in Luca's arms was like coming home. All the doubts, all the mistrust, all the hurdles along the way, were just steps she either wanted to take, or she didn't. If something was worth having, it was worth fighting for, and she had.

They had talked long into the night about the past, the present, and the future. So long as they travelled that road together, she didn't much mind what lay ahead of them. Luca had trodden a straight line since leaving Sicily, he'd told her, and sometimes, because Raoul had stayed with his father in the hope of winning his love, that road had taken a detour around the brother who had loved him and whom Luca had loved. But he was going to do everything he could to honour Raoul's memory, and Lyddie's.

'Good morning.'

'Good morning,' she whispered as he woke up. How precious these moments were after being so long apart. Luca was such a sight, even in the early morning. He was magnificent. His powerful body washed by the pearly light of dawn was sprawled across his big bed in his penthouse apartment. It was impossible to say how much she loved him. 'I've been waiting for you to wake up,' she admitted.

He opened one eye. 'Why? So we can continue discussing our plans for the island.'

She shrugged. 'I hope you don't mind, but I have other plans…'

'That's a relief,' he murmured gruffly.

Luca made love to her slowly and deeply until she came apart in his arms, and not once, but several times. They slept afterwards, and when she woke, he kissed her and smiled. 'Will you marry me? Or do I have to make love to you again?'

She laughed with sheer happiness. 'Both,' she said. 'I will marry you, but you have to make love to me first. After that you can ask me to marry you again.'

'The eternal circle?' he suggested.

'Of lovemaking and promises,' she agreed. 'I'm up for it, if you are.'

'Oh, I'm up for it,' he said.

'Can I just say—I love you so much?' She smiled into his eyes as she kissed him.

'You can say that all you want, Signorina Sanderson, soon to become Signora Tebaldi. In fact, I demand that you never get tired of saying it, as I will never tire of telling you how much I love you.'

'I can't wait to return to the island,' she admitted. I've missed it—you,' she admitted wryly, 'more than you will ever know. I'm thrilled that I finally qualified and became a gemologist like my mother, and I know she'd be proud of me, as would Lyddie and my father, but when I took that diploma in my hand, I knew that what my mother really wanted for me—for both her children, was for us to be happy, and I'd almost thrown that away.'

'Never, *cara*—'

'Yes,' Jen argued. 'I was still prepared to risk everything, including you, for the sake of pride. I was hurt and blinded by insecurity and defensiveness, and so I pushed you away, when all I wanted was to bring you close. But I couldn't admit it. I didn't have the courage to admit it. When I inherited the money and heard about your brother's plans for it from Jay-Dee, my first thought was that you must be involved. I knew that was what Raoul would want.' Her eyes fired with certainty. 'The three of us working together—'

'The two of us living together?' Luca amended with his sexy, slow-burning smile.

Jen gave him the look she had always reserved for Luca when he teased her. 'It would make the logistics of working together easier,' she agreed, teasing him back.

Suddenly the cell door wasn't just open, it had vanished. 'I love you,' she said. 'We've both learned a lot, and mostly about trust.'

'Only trust?' Luca whispered. 'What about love? I've learned a lot about love, and I'm looking forward to returning to live on an island that will ring to the sound of our children.'

He caressed her stomach and their child responded vigorously, as if in agreement.

'I need to make up for lost time,' he said bluntly. 'I need proof that you've forgiven me.'

Jen laughed. 'You'll stop at nothing,' she said.

'Too right,' Luca agreed. 'I'm hungry for you,' he explained with a rueful shrug.

'Not as hungry as I am for you, after a fast,' Jen insisted.

'I think you may have become insatiable,' he murmured, frowning as he brushed her hair aside to kiss the nape of her neck.

'I know I have,' Jen whispered, pulling him close again.

EPILOGUE

THE CEREMONY TO renew their marriage vows was always going to be a special occasion, but it didn't take long for Jen to decide that it was the best day of her life. Luci was dressed in the pale blue shorts and comfortable white linen shirt he would be wearing for the ceremony, and she loved the thought that two children would be sharing the celebration with them.

Their wedding had been an entirely different affair. Luca and she had married by special licence the same week they were reunited, so there had been no time to make elaborate arrangements, and no need for them, as both bride and groom had declared that all they needed was each other. With Shirley, Tess, and Jay-Dee as their witnesses, their wedding had been a quiet family affair with people they cared about.

Jen had worn a warm, coral-coloured maternity dress she'd bought off the peg in a sale last minute, while Luca had stunned everyone including Jen into silence by looking like Lucifer redeemed in one of his stunning dark power suits. Sweeping her into his arms and his heart, he had declared her to be the love of his life.

Today was very different, Jen mused as she led Luci by the hand into the flower-filled courtyard where their guests were waiting. Everyone cheered and applauded enthusiastically when she arrived, warming her heart and giving her every confidence for the future of the projects that she and Luca and Jay-Dee were working on together. It filled her with joy to know that she could do something practical to help the charity that had helped her so unstintingly.

'You look beautiful,' Jay-Dee told her; a sentiment echoed by Tess and Shirley, and all the many new friends she had made on the island.

Luca had insisted they must travel to Rome with Luci and their two-year-old daughter Natalia—or Tallie, as the little redhead with bubble curls was known—so Jen could finally have the gown she deserved. Pale blue lace, fitted to her almost-back-to-normal form, the dress finished at knee-length, allowing Jen the freedom to sprint, if necessary, to lift either of the teeny Tebaldis out of a scrape. And Luca had insisted that on this one occasion she should wear the Emperor's Diamond, which, far from being the curse everyone had thought it, had brought them nothing but love and happiness since the day it was set free from the dark box in which it had been kept, and exhibited in the light by Jen, for anyone who wanted to see it to admire.

Jen had three spare outfits crammed into a workman-like tote for Luci, and she still wasn't sure that would be enough to keep her rascally son looking respectable throughout the day. If there was mud to be found, Luci would find it, and given half a chance he would be under the wedding table with one of the family's dogs, sharing titbits out of his pockets. Their home in Sicily was light, bright, chaotic and wonderful, and, with the caterers having created a chocolate spectacular for the feast after today's ceremony, Jen didn't hold out high hopes that Luci would make it through the day without at least one very messy and sticky disaster.

'Is my beautiful wife ready?'

If there was a sight more spectacular than Jen's husband, dressed in relaxed linen tailoring, backlit by shimmering sunlight, holding their baby daughter securely on the wide spread of his shoulders, it could only be when Luci whooped at the sight of his *papà* and ran to launch himself into Luca's arms.

'I should start a circus act,' Luca exclaimed as he caught his son in one arm, while holding onto his daughter with the other.

'The Tumbling Tebaldis,' Jen suggested, thinking what a long way they'd come from suspicion and shadow to this beautiful light-filled courtyard in the gracious old house in Sicily, which they had transformed into a true home.

'How about *Viva For Ever* as the headline banner for our publicity?' Luca suggested with a teasing grin as he drew Jen and his children into the circle of his arms.

* * * * *

*If you enjoyed this story,
don't miss these other great reads
from Susan Stephens*

*A DIAMOND FOR DEL RIO'S HOUSEKEEPER
IN THE SHEIKH'S SERVICE
BOUND TO THE TUSCAN BILLIONAIRE
BACK IN THE BRAZILIAN'S BED*

Available now!

MILLS & BOON®
Hardback – March 2017

ROMANCE

Secrets of a Billionaire's Mistress	Sharon Kendrick
Claimed for the De Carrillo Twins	Abby Green
The Innocent's Secret Baby	Carol Marinelli
The Temporary Mrs Marchetti	Melanie Milburne
A Debt Paid in the Marriage Bed	Jennifer Hayward
The Sicilian's Defiant Virgin	Susan Stephens
Pursued by the Desert Prince	Dani Collins
The Forgotten Gallo Bride	Natalie Anderson
Return of Her Italian Duke	Rebecca Winters
The Millionaire's Royal Rescue	Jennifer Faye
Proposal for the Wedding Planner	Sophie Pembroke
A Bride for the Brooding Boss	Bella Bucannon
Their Secret Royal Baby	Carol Marinelli
Her Hot Highland Doc	Annie O'Neil
His Pregnant Royal Bride	Amy Ruttan
Baby Surprise for the Doctor Prince	Robin Gianna
Resisting Her Army Doc Rival	Susan MacKay
A Month to Marry the Midwife	Fiona McArthur
Billionaire's Baby Promise	Sarah M. Anderson
Seduce Me, Cowboy	Maisey Yates

MILLS & BOON®
Large Print – March 2017

ROMANCE

Di Sione's Virgin Mistress	Sharon Kendrick
Snowbound with His Innocent Temptation	Cathy Williams
The Italian's Christmas Child	Lynne Graham
A Diamond for Del Rio's Housekeeper	Susan Stephens
Claiming His Christmas Consequence	Michelle Smart
One Night with Gael	Maya Blake
Married for the Italian's Heir	Rachael Thomas
Christmas Baby for the Princess	Barbara Wallace
Greek Tycoon's Mistletoe Proposal	Kandy Shepherd
The Billionaire's Prize	Rebecca Winters
The Earl's Snow-Kissed Proposal	Nina Milne

HISTORICAL

The Runaway Governess	Liz Tyner
The Winterley Scandal	Elizabeth Beacon
The Queen's Christmas Summons	Amanda McCabe
The Discerning Gentleman's Guide	Virginia Heath

MEDICAL

A Daddy for Her Daughter	Tina Beckett
Reunited with His Runaway Bride	Robin Gianna
Rescued by Dr Rafe	Annie Claydon
Saved by the Single Dad	Annie Claydon
Sizzling Nights with Dr Off-Limits	Janice Lynn
Seven Nights with Her Ex	Louisa Heaton

MILLS & BOON®
Hardback – April 2017

ROMANCE

The Italian's One-Night Baby	Lynne Graham
The Desert King's Captive Bride	Annie West
Once a Moretti Wife	Michelle Smart
The Boss's Nine-Month Negotiation	Maya Blake
The Secret Heir of Alazar	Kate Hewitt
Crowned for the Drakon Legacy	Tara Pammi
His Mistress with Two Secrets	Dani Collins
The Argentinian's Virgin Conquest	Bella Frances
Stranded with the Secret Billionaire	Marion Lennox
Reunited by a Baby Bombshell	Barbara Hannay
The Spanish Tycoon's Takeover	Michelle Douglas
Miss Prim and the Maverick Millionaire	Nina Singh
Their One Night Baby	Carol Marinelli
Forbidden to the Playboy Surgeon	Fiona Lowe
A Mother to Make a Family	Emily Forbes
The Nurse's Baby Secret	Janice Lynn
The Boss Who Stole Her Heart	Jennifer Taylor
Reunited by Their Pregnancy Surprise	Louisa Heaton
The Ten-Day Baby Takeover	Karen Booth
Expecting the Billionaire's Baby	Andrea Laurence

MILLS & BOON®
Large Print – April 2017

ROMANCE

A Di Sione for the Greek's Pleasure	Kate Hewitt
The Prince's Pregnant Mistress	Maisey Yates
The Greek's Christmas Bride	Lynne Graham
The Guardian's Virgin Ward	Caitlin Crews
A Royal Vow of Convenience	Sharon Kendrick
The Desert King's Secret Heir	Annie West
Married for the Sheikh's Duty	Tara Pammi
Winter Wedding for the Prince	Barbara Wallace
Christmas in the Boss's Castle	Scarlet Wilson
Her Festive Doorstep Baby	Kate Hardy
Holiday with the Mystery Italian	Ellie Darkins

HISTORICAL

Bound by a Scandalous Secret	Diane Gaston
The Governess's Secret Baby	Janice Preston
Married for His Convenience	Eleanor Webster
The Saxon Outlaw's Revenge	Elisabeth Hobbes
In Debt to the Enemy Lord	Nicole Locke

MEDICAL

Waking Up to Dr Gorgeous	Emily Forbes
Swept Away by the Seductive Stranger	Amy Andrews
One Kiss in Tokyo...	Scarlet Wilson
The Courage to Love Her Army Doc	Karin Baine
Reawakened by the Surgeon's Touch	Jennifer Taylor
Second Chance with Lord Branscombe	Joanna Neil

MILLS & BOON®

Why shop at millsandboon.co.uk?

Each year, thousands of romance readers find their perfect read at millsandboon.co.uk. That's because we're passionate about bringing you the very best romantic fiction. Here are some of the advantages of shopping at www.millsandboon.co.uk:

* **Get new books first**—you'll be able to buy your favourite books one month before they hit the shops

* **Get exclusive discounts**—you'll also be able to buy our specially created monthly collections, with up to 50% off the RRP

* **Find your favourite authors**—latest news, interviews and new releases for all your favourite authors and series on our website, plus ideas for what to try next

* **Join in**—once you've bought your favourite books, don't forget to register with us to rate, review and join in the discussions

Visit **www.millsandboon.co.uk** for all this and more today!